What Do You Know of My Soul?

A novel by

Mary Paynter

ISBN: **1494381435**
ISBN-13: **978-1494381431**

DEDICATION

for Maureen Phillips, Ida Bell, and Carol Rotz,

and inspiring teachers everywhere.

Soli Dei Gloria

"What can you ever really know of other people's souls — of their temptations, their opportunities, their struggles?"

-C.S Lewis, *Mere Christianity*

Part I: Arriving

He came through the gloom, a
Silent shadow sliding through the green cathedrals of
Breathing trees. Pausing, he scented the air,
Nostrils flaring, and dark eyes swimming with the
Deeper shades of leaf and bole. The eyes grew
Wide, the muscled body froze, the scent of
Cat became a velvet thing that turned, and
Gazed with hooded eyes of golden fire at those of the one
Who stood and sweat his involuntary fear.
Whiskered lips wrinkled in a silent snarl, but
The silken fur gleamed with the blood of a recent kill. A full belly
Called for sleep, and the velvet thing moved in
Majesty to hidden chambers.

He stood still in his sweat, and appetite
Was numbed by the stone in his gut.
He wanted only to turn and flee to his lair,
But the face of his woman, young and patient, her swollen belly,
Moved uncomplaining to the fluid screens of his mind.
He grunted his disgust at the fear that had
Turned him back to a child. Hunter and hunt
Were resumed. Something died. The woman with child
Ate, and was satisfied, and looked on her
Man, and was satisfied. He, the hunter, did obeisance
To his gods.

As the plane left Atlanta, Annie strained to see the vanishing city.

"This your first trip outside the US?" asked the woman in the next seat.

The girl blushed a little. "Yes, ma'am," she said. "Farthest I've been before was to college in Kansas."

"You on vacation?"

"No, ma'am, I'm going to teach the children at a little village school. I'm... I'm like a missionary," she explained diffidently, wondering if she should tell people or if she should keep it as a kind of secret; she thought they might withdraw and treat her differently when they heard. The woman looked her over, taking in the air of anxiety and the newness of her clothes; *K-mart, probably*, she thought. *Poor kid doesn't know what she's in for.*

"I've been home to see my mother and catch up on the latest nieces and nephews. My husband's in oil exploration. We do this trip all the time. You kinda get used to it. Like you get used to the way of life out there in Bangita. The city's okay, you can get most of what you need, but I don't know about those little places." She looked sharply at the younger woman. "Do you have a good support system? I mean, are there folks out there to meet you and show you the ropes 'n that?"

"Oh yes, ma'am, we have a good organization! There are other missionaries there already, they're meeting me at the airport and everything, and I'll be getting a salary from the US and all that too." She felt annoyed. This woman was starting to remind her of some of the folks at her church, always talking about the "third world" with a mixture of contempt and trepidation. Then she remembered her college anthropology class, and a familiar tickle of fear and uncertainty started up somewhere under her diaphragm.

Annie looked at her travel companion. She looked tired, with lines around her mouth that deepened as she relaxed and closed her eyes briefly. Her soft dark hair was neatly bobbed. At least this woman had lived there. She must know what she was talking about. The woman opened her eyes and saw that she was being inspected; a hint of suspicion showed on her face as her eyebrows lifted in query.

Annie found herself blushing again. "I'm sorry – I've never met someone who has actually lived in Bangita. Please tell me about it - is it really so different? Oh, I'm Annie," and she put out her hand.

The woman's face softened and she smiled and took her hand. She patted Annie's hand with her left one. "Alicia Williams. And it sure is different. O-oh yes, more'n you can guess at, honey!" Alicia settled comfortably into her seat for several hours of conversation on one of her favorite topics: just how different things were in Bangita.

The runway was scarred, but although the airport was small there were signs that maintenance did happen, however erratically. A few dusty palm trees drooped limply near the terminal building, and bright orange, purple, and cerise bougainvillea romped enthusiastically over the perimeter fence. The air felt as wet and heavy as a soggy towel, and over all hung a smell of hot earth, salt water, and drying fish. Baggage was hauled out of the airplane holds and lined up on the runway for passengers to claim. Annie found her bags and dragged them into a heap. She had her guitar, a heavy book bag, and a hard-shell case with her breakables in it, besides her cabin baggage and a huge wheeled bag of clothing. It really hadn't seemed that much at home... She looked at the daunting pile, and then measured the distance to the airport building, a hundred yards of heat-shimmered concrete. She felt the sweat trickle down her spine and wiped it from her forehead and upper lip. She thought of a cold drink and air conditioning inside.

Alicia Williams came up with her cabin bag slung over her shoulder and pulling a wheeled bag. "Well, honey, you're gonna have to learn to travel lighter. Still, I guess this is your first trip." She grabbed Annie's guitar and headed for the building, disregarding her faint protests. Another passenger, an American in a light tropical suit, looked over and shook his head, clicking his tongue with suppressed irritation. He had a briefcase strapped to his wheeled carry-on. He came over and picked up Annie's hard-shell suitcase, ignoring her protests, and following Alicia Williams' determined back. Annie valiantly got her remaining baggage under control and struggled after them, feeling humiliated by her inadequacy.

It felt slightly cooler inside the tiny airport building, out of the glaring sun, but the crush of passengers and those meeting them hopelessly overwhelmed whatever air conditioner may have been at work. The heat was rivaled by the din of greetings, queries and replies, and announcements in Bangese and heavily accented, incomprehensible English over a PA system that whistled and squawked like short-wave radio. There was no sign of any kind of restaurant or even a vending machine. Annie saw the American who had taken her bag leave it near the entry gate and make his way through the crush to the customs desk. He was clearly well known, for the official smiled broadly when he saw him. They exchanged affable greetings. She watched the American hand over his passport. The customs official opened the passport, took from it a folded piece of paper, and checked the photograph casually. He handed it back and waved the man through.

"That's the way it's done, just put a good-sized bill in your passport and you'll be through," said a comfortable voice at her shoulder. Alicia Williams was watching the same scene.

"I can't do that! It's bribery and we're not allowed to - it's illegal and ... and... Hey, that's my bag!" as someone picked up the bag left by the American man at the gate. "Stop! Hey!" she yelled angrily. She tried to go after him, realized she was abandoning the rest of her luggage, and stopped, helpless with indecision.

"Go on, honey, I'll watch your things!" Alicia flapped her hand to urge her away.

She pushed forward into the crowd, which closed around her in a wave of hot bodies for whom deodorant was not a consideration. She felt herself carried forward on a sea, the tide flowing towards the exit. Ahead of her she could see the head of the man who had taken her suitcase, an ordinary dark head in an ocean of dark heads. He walked unhindered out the door, though she tried to call out for someone to stop him. Other faces turned and scowled at her in annoyance as she pushed through the crowd, stepping on toes, trying to elbow her way through. Finally she reached the door and ran into the towering bulk of a uniformed man.

"Stop, miss! You cannot go out. First, customs, then taxi."

"But that man - he has my suitcase! There he is! He's getting into that taxi - please let me go after him! You stop him then - please help me," and she tried to push past him. He grabbed her arm. His eyes were hard and black with anger.

"You will go through customs! All foreigners must go through customs!" He propelled her back through the crowd, against the tide to the customs desk, his grip painfully tight on her wrist. "Check this one," he said to the official standing there, and to Annie, "Where is your baggage?"

"Over there," she pointed to where Alicia Williams still stood with the rest of her things. He pushed her over that way and, still holding her arm, helped her to drag her belongings over to the desk. Alicia went ahead of them with her one bag and was waved through. Annie fumbled one-handed for her passport.

"Can't you let me go now?" she asked angrily, trying to pull her arm away. She looked up into the face of the door official and saw an expression she could not read in his shuttered eyes. The grip on her arm tightened. She could see Alicia Williams' face, blank of expression. She acted unconcerned, but there was a warning in her eyes.

Reality began to penetrate through Annie's frustration. A wash of fear suddenly extinguished her anger. Her face felt stiff, but she tried to smile as she handed over her passport. "I am so sorry," she said. "I thought someone had taken my suitcase. I guess I was mistaken."

The customs official grunted and opened the passport. His face grew still and he narrowed his eyes to hide the glint in them as he slid two folded bills from the passport. He glanced at the information inside and checked the photo's likeness. Annie's short blonde bob and blue eyes seemed as unusual here as a tree in Antarctica. Still he thumbed slowly through the whole book, carefully reading pages bare of any stamps or entries. He looked for a long time at the visa, and then slowly and deliberately placed his official stamp on five separate and blank pages before handing the book back to her. One by one her bags and suitcases were hauled onto the desk and carefully sifted through. Items of clothing were unfolded and shaken out, containers opened and their contents poked into with a pen, and everything stuffed back at random. The bags were forced shut. The guard from the door released her arm.

"Welcome to Bangita," he said, with a small, formal bow.

Outside on the steaming sidewalk, Alicia Williams asked softly,

"Are you okay?"

No, she wasn't okay at all. She felt physically violated. The pain in her throbbing arm heightened her internal sense of loss and devastation. Her shock was too great for tears.

"Did you put that money in my passport?" she whispered.

"Yes, I did. Now don't you be mad at me, honey. You could have ended up in prison."

The girl began to scrabble frantically in her purse. Alicia saw what she was doing and said, "I used your money to pay them. You don't owe me anything. Now where's your ride? Are you taking a taxi to town? You can ride with me if you need to."

Alicia stepped off the sidewalk and began to wave her hand and yell, "Taxi! Taxi!" A dirty and dented car pulled on to the curb. Once red, it was now faded and scratched, mottled with rust and bird droppings. The driver leaped out and began loading luggage into the trunk. He looked inquiringly at the women and gestured towards Annie's baggage.

"Well, honey, are you coming?"

"I don't know what to do - I'd better wait here like I'm meant to. I just can't think what could have held them up - I'm sure they wouldn't have forgotten," she said helplessly.

Alicia shook her head with an affectionate smile. "Didn't you hear anything I told you? Anything can happen in this place - and probably will. Here, you take my husband's card, and call if you need us." With a sudden flash of sympathy on her face, she stepped forward and hugged the girl. "I'm really not sure I should leave you here alone."

"It's okay, Ms Alicia, really. I'm sure they'll be here soon. You go right ahead, I'll be fine."

The woman looked dubious, but the taxi driver looked as if he might be trying to find someone else to cram into his car. "Alright, honey, I'll go, but if they don't come soon then you get a taxi to that address on the card I gave you, okay?"

As Annie watched the taxi drive away, she wanted to run after them and yell, *Stop, stop! Take me with you!* Tears burned at the back of her eyes, and she blew her nose angrily, despising her weakness and refusing to give in. She took a deep breath and looked around her. The parking lot was almost completely empty, the crowd from the plane having dispersed long before. A few cars were huddled in the meager shade of palm trees. She walked out to the end of the sidewalk and found herself at the top of a steep, rocky slope.

The airport was located on an elevated promontory on the southern end of the island. In the distance she could see great white, yellow, and coral pink hotels like cruise ships on the curved shoreline of a wide bay. Little winks of sunlight reflected off cars traveling along the foreshore. Below where she stood, a broad stretch of white beach curved away towards the south. The light onshore breeze was laden with salt and the pungent smell of the racks of drying fish and fishnets that staggered in ramshackle array along the beach, between scattered boats where groups of men gathered, working and talking. Women haggled and bargained loudly at the tables of fish sellers and walked away with baskets on their heads, their purchases wrapped in broad banana leaves. The men wore ragged cut-off jeans or shorts, their mahogany torsos gleaming with sweat and salt water. The women wore shabby cotton print dresses or tee-shirts over wrapped cloth skirts. Many of the swarming, scrambling, chattering children wore only a T-shirt, or a tattered pair of shorts. The youngest were naked. Annie stood and watched, fascinated. An image flashed through her mind of herself teaching these half-naked children, and doubt quirked an eyebrow at her.

She became aware of a small group of children hovering nearby, whispering and scuffling and pointing at her. She smiled at them, timidly, and raised her hand in a small wave. They giggled furiously, pushing at each other to make someone else be the first to approach her. Finally, one of the children (a girl? - she had on what looked like a ragged pair of cut-off bib overalls) edged over timidly.

"'Allo!" she offered shyly.

"Hello! What's your name? I am Annie."

At this the children howled with terror and glee, and began to chant, "An-nee! An-nee!" at the top of their voices. She crouched down to look them in the eye, and they approached her with all the caution of a street cur, expecting the worst and hoping for the best. She took a little naked toddler onto her lap and again was assailed with howls, this time of delight, and the entire group flung themselves at her with such exuberance that she was knocked flat and found herself sitting in the dirt covered with laughing children. She tried to hug them all, opening her arms and gathering them in. Finally she was able to get them lined up in some sort of order on her lap and at her side.

Now what? She wondered. *Will they understand if I tell them a story?*

She decided to sing a song instead, and picked the silliest one she could think of, one that included pulling faces and making weird noises. The children loved it, quickly learning to imitate her, and they were on to their third noisy chorus when a Land Rover pulled up in a cloud of dust, and a thin, wiry white man got out and came over to her. The children went still and quiet when they saw him, and the more timid among them scrambled up and stood at a little distance as he approached.

"Are you Annie Robbins?" he asked curtly. He wore silver-rimmed glasses and seemed harassed and worried.

She scrambled out from under the pile of children and held out her hand, then quickly wiped it on her skirt before holding it out again. "Yes, sir, I am."

He shook her hand. "Tom Palmer. Missionary. You know, we wrote. I'm sorry I'm late; I was held up at the Agriculture Department down town. I should have known - anyway that's just how it is around here and you'll get used to it. That your stuff?" He indicated the diminished pile of her baggage, still over on the sidewalk.

"Yes, that's it. Um - there was another one, I had another suitcase, but it was - stolen..."

He looked at her, frowning. "You'd better tell me about that in the car. I need to get back to the office."

He climbed back into the Land Rover, hurriedly backed it up to the pile of bags, and began to sling them into the back. Annie felt torn between her need to appear competent and efficient, and the bottomless hunger she saw in the great brown eyes that stared wistfully at her. Kneeling in the dust, she put out her arms and six ragged little bodies pressed into them. She felt the tears sting her eyes as she saw the running sores, running noses, the dirt, the rags, and above all the terrible desperation for love, for someone to love and hold and cherish them.

"I will come back to see you," she promised impulsively, meaning it, feeling their lost vulnerability.

The children stood still and silent, gazing at Annie with blank faces. Tom Palmer was in the Land Rover. He started it up and drove over to where she stood. She climbed into the passenger seat on the left side of the car, and waved her hand at the small knot of children. Annie watched in the rear view mirror as Palmer drove away. Even when she could no longer see them, she knew they had not moved.

Palmer glanced across at her. "My wife can take you down town tomorrow to report your stolen bag. Do you have insurance?"

"Uh… I took out some travel insurance, but I think it was only for the actual trip."

"Well you can go down and report it anyway. Not much chance of getting any of it back, but you never know."

"Thank you," said Annie awkwardly. This tense stranger was not what she had expected – though she wasn't sure what she *had* expected. He cleared his throat, as though he realized that he had forgotten good manners.

"I'm sorry – I've been a bit abrupt. Things are pretty tough out here; it seems like nothing goes smoothly some days. I guess you're having one of those too." He glanced over at her and she saw his expression soften. "I will be taking you to our home for a couple of days at first; just so we can help you get settled in and adjusted a bit. My wife will be glad of the company."

The following afternoon, Mrs. Palmer took Annie downtown to report the theft of her suitcase. The police station was her second lesson in Bangese politics. Mrs. Palmer demonstrated how *not* to achieve your objective with Bangese officialdom, and Annie began to fear they would be arrested as the older woman haughtily demanded in English that an officer be sent immediately to investigate this crime, all the while denouncing the shocking rate of criminal activity in Bangita amid implications regarding the inefficiency of the country's police. They were saved by the arrival of a young man whose dark hair had a red gleam. His blue eyes were startling against his tan, and twinkled mischievously as he flashed them a broad grin.

"Good day, Officer Ganza!" he said in Bangese, "Are these ladies causing you some trouble?"

The long-suffering policeman glared at the women and launched into voluble Bangese that Annie could barely follow, a frustrated rant about foreigners who think everything must be done their way, who don't realize they are not in their country now, and that things here are done in the Bangese way, and they have so much stuff anyway, they shouldn't even miss a single suitcase –

"May I be of service to you, ladies?" The young man turned to them, and the official flow of Bangese behind the counter subsided into a stream of muttering as papers were shuffled and ordered and stamped and scored in angry pencil. "Mrs. Palmer, I have not had the pleasure of meeting this delightful young woman. I am Ben Grant. At your service." He took the hand she offered him and bowed low, lightly touching her hand with his lips. She withdrew it awkwardly, flattered and embarrassed, and as his eyes met hers, she saw the gleam of laughter and realized that he was deliberately providing the distraction they needed to defuse the situation.

"I'm Annie," she started, but Mrs. Palmer cut in abruptly.

"This is Annie Robbins," she said briskly. "She is a missionary teacher, here to work for my husband," and the warning in her eyes was unmistakable. "Thank you, Ben, but we're done here now." She swept from the room. Annie smiled and shrugged apologetically and went after her, and knew that his eyes followed her.

Later, in the car, she tried asking casually about him; where did Mrs. Palmer know him from?

"His family goes to our church. His father works at the American Embassy downtown, but his mother is Bangese. Really I don't know why people do that. Mixed marriages are just doomed from the start. Just look at that boy, neither fish nor fowl."

"Ummm, I'm not sure what you mean, ma'am."

Ada Palmer shot her a look that was part surprise, part scorn. "Well, technically he's American I suppose, but really, he's also Bangese, though the Bangese don't really accept his kind either. Well, really, I mean, don't people realize what their children will have to go through? If they MUST marry across the color line like that, they really shouldn't have any children. They just never fit in."

Annie lapsed into silence. A tiny chill crept into a small corner of her soul.

They pulled into a parking area outside a small modern office block. A sign announced that these were the offices of Doctors Such-and-Such, part of a medical group that Annie recognized from home, a large organization that, among other things, ran busy abortion clinics.

"Do they allow abortion here?" she asked, surprised.

"Yes, they do – the new government that came in a few years ago wanted to have an up-to-date constitution, and it's pretty liberal. It seems that the bad parts of Western culture get absorbed along with the good. It's like the movies and TV shows they show here – the worst possible sort that shows the US in such a bad light. It's no wonder some people think America is so decadent!

"I have an appointment for my annual checkup at the doctor's. I would have cancelled but you have to wait weeks for an appointment – there are just so few decent women's doctors in this place," she sighed with a mixture of irritation and resignation. "So I'm afraid I will have to ask you to wait with me till I get through."

"Since we're so close to the stores in the main street, I'll just take a walk, ma'am. I'm so excited to be able to see everything at last!"

"Well I'm not sure that's a good idea, Annie. There are so many things that could happen - I don't think I should let you go off by yourself! I feel quite responsible for you. I would hate for something to happen."

"I'm sure I'll be fine, Ms. Ada. I have the office address written down anyway so I can ask if I get lost," Annie said, and she showed her a little notebook with the address scribbled quickly in the margin.

"Well, as long as you don't go far now, and you be sure to be back here by three-thirty. I would hate for you to be out in this city on your own when it starts to get dark. Once the rush hour starts there are all sorts of people about and you just don't know who you can trust." Ada Palmer looked worried, showing the frustration she felt at having an urgent appointment on one hand and a stubborn young woman on the other. "I'm sure to be finished at the doctor's quite quickly. Are you sure you don't want to just wait for me?"

"No, no, I'll be fine on my own. Don't worry; I'll be back in time, Ms. Ada. See you later!" Annie walked off quickly before the older woman could think of any other reason to delay her. Surely she meant well, but she seemed suffocating in her paranoia. Annie wanted to see and touch and taste and smell the new place she found herself in. What was the point of coming to a new country if you spent all your time in a closed world of your own culture, sanitized and prepackaged?

Outside the gate and the high iron fence of the American medical building, the sun was warm on her cheek and she could smell the salt ocean on the breeze. There were other smells too, some a lot less than pleasant. She passed drifts of trash in the gutters, and once she saw a dead rat. Empty cans, bottles, and food wrappers lay everywhere, especially around the overflowing garbage cans. The main road was full of business-suited hurrying people, office buildings, and stores with fashion mannequins in the windows. *Imagine the Gap being here*, she thought, staring at the storefront across the street. The clothes in the window looked much the same as those back home. *Well*, she thought, *that's not what I came for...* She turned down a side street and found smaller stores with unusual items for sale, crafts and baskets, and beautifully dyed cloth. Still the price tags showed more than she felt able to pay, and she wandered on. A lovely shaded park attracted her, and she crossed the street to walk along its pathways. Little groups of people sat or lay about on the grass. A group of gray-haired men played a game that looked like checkers. They grumbled and cursed at one another, and bursts of laughter greeted every witty insult. Strange-looking green pigeons pecked at the crumbs and litter around wire trash baskets. She saw an enormous orange-headed lizard run up a tree.

She passed across the street alongside whitewashed older buildings that she thought must be survivors of colonial times. Through a wrought-iron gate she glimpsed a shaded stone-paved patio, where a fountain splashed amid palm trees and the cooing of the green pigeons. She stood a long time and gazed into another world, whose comings and goings she could only guess at.

Around a corner she found herself at a busy road, where buses, ancient pickup trucks, and battered minivans, bulging with passengers and mountains of baggage, roared and growled between throngs of pedestrians. Across the road was a loud and noisy market place. As she slipped among the shoppers and stalls, she didn't notice how people stared at a lone white girl. She stopped to look over some hand-dyed fabrics and tried out her Bangese on the middle-aged, tired-looking woman behind the table.

"How much is this?" she asked, holding up a folded piece of blue cloth with a soft, random-dyed pattern.

"Ten dollar," said the woman.

"Bangese dollars?"

"American. Forty Bangese dollar. For you, I give you two for ten American," the woman said, and there was a little gleam in her eye as she held up another folded piece of cloth, this one in a strawberry pink shade.

"Okay, I'll take them," said Annie, and pulled out the ten. As she walked away she realized she was the object of obsequious attention from every stall holder. If she stopped to pick up something, she was immediately assailed with cries from surrounding sellers about how much better and cheaper their wares were than the ones she had in her hand, until eventually her head was spinning with the chaos. Suddenly a cheery voice yelled out behind her.

"Hey, Annie! What are you doing here?"

She looked around, surprised and relieved to hear her name. There was Ben, their rescuer from the police station, sitting on a small motor scooter, beckoning to her. "Want a ride?"

"Sure, thanks. That would be great!" She ran over and climbed on the back of the scooter, suddenly eager to get away from there. "Don't I need a helmet?"

"No, you're fine! Where to?" he yelled above the noise of the vehicles all around them.

"Dr. Jones' office," she yelled back, and a wave of exhilaration swept over her as she hung on, her hair blowing and a huge grin on her face, as he wove rapidly in and out of the chaotic traffic.

"What are you doing tomorrow?" he asked as she climbed off the scooter outside the doctor's office.

"I'm not too sure, but I think they want me to help out at the mission offices."

"I know where the offices are. How about I come around there and take you out for lunch? Say, twelve-thirty?"

"That sounds great! I'd like that – thank you!" she exclaimed, and suddenly, as she looked into his happy, handsome face, Annie felt herself blushing, to her confusion and ever greater embarrassment, so that the cause and the effect exacerbated each other, and she said, "Uh, okay, 'bye then," and turned away to hurry into the medical office building, almost running into Ada Palmer as she was coming out.

She could not know how far that blush went to securing her interest in Ben's thoughts. She missed entirely the disapproving look that crossed Mrs. Palmer's face when she saw Ben pulling away into the traffic.

Email: June

Hey Charlie!

How are you? And how is Aunt Ginny doing? I am safe and sound in Bangita. The flight was good, though sooo long. I had a lady from Atlanta sitting next to me who told me all about life in BC – that's what they call Bangita City around here. Her name is Alicia Williams and her husband works for the oil company. I'll be staying with the missionaries here, the Palmers, for a while. Mrs. Palmer has taken me shopping and sightseeing. And of course we have been to church. The Palmers visit different churches each week so that they can stay in touch with everyone, and not be accused of favoritism. The church we went to this past week is so different than we're used to at home. The people really sing and they clap and stamp their feet. Also, the men and boys sit on one side of the church, and the women and girls on the other. I'm feeling a bit overwhelmed with all the new people I have been meeting.

BC is a lot more sophisticated than I thought it would be, though there are people walking everywhere and the traffic is crazy, too. There's great stuff in the stores that seems quite cheap to me, yet there is so much poverty, poor people begging on the streets, little kids without proper clothes or shoes. I find myself giving money to people in the street all the time, even though people tell me not to. Back home I thought I was quite poor... I knew wealth was a relative thing but here that seems more obvious than ever.

The Bangese people are lovely, the girls so pretty and petite. Everyone has dark hair and skin and eyes and I stick out like a sore thumb being so fair. Sometimes people stare, specially the kids. It can get embarrassing! And they don't always understand me either, because of the accent. I asked for water in a restaurant and the girl said they didn't have any! I was so surprised but then Mrs. Palmer said "water" the way they say it here and they got me some. Sometimes I feel dumb because I don't know what to call something in a way that people will understand. I mean, they speak English, but it's a different kind of English.

I'm hoping to go soon to Kinta village to start the school – it's about five hours from here, up in the mountains and the jungle. I hope my Bangese is going to be okay - I hardly use it here in the city because most people speak English. There seems to be a problem with getting me up there – I don't know what that's about.

While I'm still in town I will be able to email but there's no power up in the village, so you can write me at the mission address. Mr. Palmer will bring mail to me at the village about once a month, and bring my letters back here with him for mailing. I will let you know when I leave.

Love and miss you already,
Your 'baby' sister,
Annie

Part II: Change

The pain was a spear in her gut, tooth and
Claw tearing at her back and thighs. No
Mother was there to comfort or help with this, her
First child. She writhed and gasped and the man
Crouched helpless, in fear for her pain, in fear
Of the sounds of her, the smell of her blood, in the
Unforgiving thickets. Monkeys had fled in fright at the
Terrible groaning, the screams barely stifled.
All around the living things of the forest sensed
Impending doom, the horror of blood and death,
And crept silent to hiding places where death might not
Find them when it came for her. With a final whimper of
Helpless torment she fell limp against the tree
Where he had laid her. He saw little feet, covered with
Blood. Pulled at them, gingerly at first but with growing
Desperation, watching the life pump from his woman
In a crimson stream. With a howl of helpless rage he
Pulled, ripped the little body from the mother's womb
In a flood of blood and amniotic fluid. The dying woman
Groaned faintly. The eyes fluttered open, stared sightless
At the man kneeling there, covered in her blood, the body
Of their child still in his hands. A shudder, and a long, deep sigh.
Her eyes grew glassy.

He started up in horror of the dead thing before him, and
Dropped the child. It mewed, a tiny pitiful cry, and he
Snatched it up again and stared at the wrinkled face
Cradled in his bloodied hand. The eyes opened, tiny
Windows to the light of cruel day, and the head turned
To nuzzle hungrily at the base of his thumb. His limbs shook as

Waves of powerful emotion ripped like storm winds
Through his inner being. He clutched the baby to his naked breast,
And lifted his head to howl his rage and anguish.

In a distant lair, golden eyes narrowed and furred ears
Swiveled to catch the sound.

The scent of death hung heavy in the gold-green grove.
Small scavengers drew nearer.

The hunter slipped through the shadows. Across his chest hung
A small bundle wrapped in a soft monkey-skin. In his heart hung his
Pain, heavy as a fallen tree, dark as the night,
Raw as a wound.

They had lunch at a bustling Bangese restaurant. She ate food that Ben suggested she order, Bangese specialties, things she didn't recognize, new flavors that grew in complexity and pleasure on her tongue. The lively conversation of Bangese office workers, young couples, and some young people who looked like college students, flowed in a melodic hum around them, while local pop music played in the background.

"Thank you so much for bringing me here! This is so amazing. The real thing!" Annie looked around and drank it in with all her senses. Turning to him, she said, "Tell me about your family, your work, where did you go to school – I want to know everything."

"Oh yes, and why would you want to know everything about me?" Ben sat back in his chair and grinned at her.

"Well you can just call it cultural research. I'm interviewing a real Bangese person for the first time. So fire away!"

His face grew momentarily more serious. "Well some people would tell you that I'm not a real Bangese at all, since my father is American."

"How did your parents meet each other?"

"Dad took a vacation from the embassy at the end of his first year. That was his first mistake – he stayed here to explore the country instead of going back home like a good lad. Anyway to hear my dad tell it, this bearded beach-bum type of guy arrived in Mom's hometown on the other side of the island in a beat-up little sailing boat, and she took pity on him and married him because no one else would have him. *She* says, though, that the red beard and blue eyes were just the first of his many charms, and that like a pirate of old, he sailed into port and stole away her heart's treasure."

"That's so romantic! She sounds like a poet. So that's where your red hair and blue eyes come from?"

"From Dad, yes, and also from some mysterious great grandfather who did a similar thing but didn't live long enough for anyone to know who he was or where he came from. Apparently, my great grandmother married a sailing foreigner, who then died of malaria before she gave birth to their first child. They say she was so beautiful that even with the encumbrance of the foreigner's child, the local chief's son was so smitten with her that he married her and raised the child as his own. They never had any sons together, just

23

three daughters, hence the elevated status of my grandfather, my mother's father. He inherited the chieftaincy, though he had to fight off a couple of cousins, from what I understand. Okay, your turn – how on earth did you come to be sitting in this restaurant with me in Bangita City?"

"You invited me, remember? And brought me here in your very own chariot too."

"Very funny. Now tell."

"Well, I thought for a long time I wanted to be a missionary or something, do something about the problems in the world instead of just complaining about them. Make a difference. We used to talk about it in college a lot, but I guess I just took it more seriously than other people. I was good at languages so I thought, if I became a teacher, I could go to a poor country and teach and make a difference that way. So I guess that's the whole story in a nutshell. Well of course there's more to it than just that.

"I found this job on the Internet and applied when I was still at college, and the missionary agency wanted me to come right away but of course I had to finish school first. They were okay with that. Bangita's kind of an out-of-the-way place; even the tourists that come here are the adventurous kind that likes to go off the beaten track. Maybe that's me too, wanting to go somewhere none of my friends had even heard of. They all had families worrying about them and hooking them up with various people they knew to get them good jobs with decent salaries and so on. Not me!" she threw back her head and laughed heartily, and he thought he had never met a girl who could laugh so freely about something that presumably wasn't that funny.

"What about your family? Don't they worry about you too?" He was puzzled.

"I don't have much of a family, really. Just my older brother and our Aunt Ginny, who's in a nursing home. Our parents were killed in a small plane accident when I was twelve. My dad was a pilot and they often took off together for a weekend here and there. They were struck by lightning up in the Rocky Mountains. It was just a freak accident. Aunt Ginny took us in. She never married and she raised us as if we were her own children. She is really my dad's aunt, so she's pretty old now, but she's our last living relative and she's very dear to us. And that's it!"

"She's in a nursing home? How did that happen?"

"She lost part of a foot because of diabetes, so she was in a wheelchair, and she had been planning on moving there anyway, so she insisted I go away to college so she could 'remain independent' as she put it. She has her own apartment and regular care from nurses and doctors; she can eat in the dining room if she wants to... I know it seems strange to some people, but that's how she wanted it. Why do you ask?"

"People here always keep their older relatives at home, it's just a thing we do. The only people in nursing homes are those with no one to care for them."

They sat and looked at each other, liking what they saw, thinking about what they had just heard. Finally Ben said, "I am trying to imagine having only two living relatives... I shall have to take you home to Buc Bay to meet my mom's people some time."

"Buc Bay? I don't think I've heard of that."

"Better known as Buccaneer Bay, the original home of pirates and privateers and all sorts of unsavory characters. See, Mrs. Palmer has plenty of good reasons for thinking you shouldn't hang out with me."

"What makes you think she doesn't think I should hang out with you?"

He leaned forward across the table, a semi-serious look on his face. "Before I tell you that, I have a confession to make: I have dated other girls before I met you. There, now you know," and he leaned back again as if resigned to being rejected instantly.

"Oh wow, I am so shocked! I shall have to leave immediately!" She feigned melodramatic horror and they both laughed. She saw him relax again and realized that it might have been a real issue. "What does that have to do with Mrs. Palmer?"

"Some of the girls I dated went to our church and there was an agreement between the ladies that the American girls were to be 'warned' if I got too close to them. Some of the girls took it as a challenge to defy their mothers but in the end I found out that I was just being used as the 'bad boy' to annoy other teenagers' parents and that didn't go over very well with me."

"Well, I'm not a teenager any more, and Mrs. Palmer isn't my mother, so I guess I don't have anyone to annoy."

"Well in that case, would you like to spend the day exploring the wonders of Bangita City with me on Saturday?"

On Saturday he came bright and early.

"So, where are we going?"

"I have some ideas, but first, is there any place you'd like to go?"

She was surprised and touched by his question. Instinctively she felt she could tell him about the children at the airport. She had tried to bring up the idea of going back to see them with Mrs. Palmer and was quickly overridden by common sense and the necessity for some other pressing task.

"Well, there were these kids I met at the airport the day I arrived, they were just sort of hanging around there, and I told them I would come back. I guess it's dumb. Maybe they won't even be there, but I'd like to go see if I can find them again. Maybe take them some candy or something...?" she trailed off at the odd little grin on his face. "What?"

"I don't think I've ever met a girl who wanted to do something like that. It will be an honor. Madam, your carriage awaits." He swept a melodramatic arm in the direction of his little Jeep. "Please note, it has been washed and had the trash removed from the floor especially for your comfort and luxury."

They climbed, laughing, into the open car and headed out. Ben glanced over and enjoyed the sight of her hair blowing in the wind as they drove. The Jeep handled well but he knew he was probably driving too fast down the steep avenue into town. He also knew that his father would have something to say about trying to impress girls but at the moment he didn't care. He really did want to impress her. After all, there must have been men back home that had ways and means of impressing women, if the TV could be believed... how was he to compete? All he had was who he was, and he fiercely wanted it to be enough. He felt he had never met someone like this, who seemed generous and caring, innocent even. An odd word came into his mind: she seemed somehow *clean,* in ways that had nothing to do with soap and water.

When they arrived at the airport, the parking lot was almost deserted again. Only two international flights were scheduled in and out on any given day, though there were also a few light planes and helicopters that ferried people and goods to some smaller outlying islands. They parked near where the ground dropped away towards the ocean, and watched the fishermen and their families working and playing along the beach.

"Do your mom's people still live like this?" asked Annie.

"Some of them do, yes, but Buc Bay is quite a tourist destination, so there are a lot of resorts and hotels there, and the cruise ships dock there too, so most of my cousins work in the shops or the hotels, and my aunts and uncles own some of them, so some of them have plenty of money. There's a pretty tight family network. I sometimes think I'd like to live there with them and other times I feel like it would be stifling. Still it's always good to go visit."

"It sounds amazing. I can't even imagine having cousins, let alone being related to half the town," she said as she scanned the beach and the area around the parking lot. "I don't see my little kids at all. Do you think they're in school?"

"Well it is Saturday, so there's no school today, but anyway I doubt it. They wouldn't be able to afford to go to school."

"They have to pay for school? Why?"

"It's really not expensive, about two dollars a month, plus they have to buy shoes and a uniform and books and stuff like that. But some of these kids don't have parents taking care of them, or their parents don't see the need for them to go to school when they will just become fishermen like their fathers. In fact if they do go to school then chances are they will want to do something different, and the parents feel like they have lost their kids then."

Annie was silent, trying to wrap her mind around these strange ideas about school. Pictures of yellow school buses and book bags and the smells of new books and pencils flashed through her mind, and she shook her head, baffled.

"Okay," she said, "they're not in school, so where could they be?"

Ben fidgeted awkwardly with the car keys, and she saw his hesitation as he answered her. "Umm, well, they could have been rounded up and taken to the homes."

"What homes? What do you mean?"

"It's a mess, it's one of the things that everyone tries to hush up, and there doesn't seem to be a good solution." He turned towards her and she saw that he was really bothered by what he was telling her. "What they do is they come around and pick up street kids. It's like rounding up dogs for the pound. Then they take them to these orphanages and feed and clothe them and keep them there for a while. Some of them, their parents come and claim them because they were just hanging out with the street kids for the day; the rest stay there for a while. If they've been there for a few weeks and no one has claimed them, they get farmed out to foster parents. The people who started it meant well, and it sounds great, until you find out that most of the so-called foster parents are basically slave traders who use these kids to work in factories or on farms or even in brothels. Some of them get sold to adoptive parents overseas – those are the lucky ones."

"Sold? Surely that's not legal?"

"Well, no, technically it's not, but there aren't enough funds available to really do anything about it, and the kids are off the streets, and so the government turns a blind eye. And then the people involved have developed great lawyer-speak for explaining away what's happening, so the whistle-blowers get nowhere."

Annie sat silent, staring at him as she tried to process what he was saying. The faces of the little ones she had met came into her mind, and as she imagined these things happening to them, tears welled up in her eyes. "This is horrible," she muttered. "Can't anyone do anything?"

He shook his head silently, his face troubled. "People are trying, though they don't achieve very much. There's a woman called Mama Deem who takes in street kids whenever they come to her. You'd like her."

"How do you know her?"

"Some of us from our church go to her house to have Sunday school with her kids. We take food for the kids and collect clothes for them, things like that. She's a pretty amazing old lady."

"Can I meet her? Do you think my kids might be with her?"

"I don't know if they are there. I suppose it's possible. But I can't take you there – she lives in Falaga. It's the worst part of Bangita City, the slums over by the garbage dumps. It's no place for someone like you."

Annie stiffened, and he saw her face close down. "Someone like me? And how is that? Female? A persnickety foreigner? Or what -?"

"For crying out loud - I'm not trying to insult you! The place is filthy, and it's not safe. And it's not like you could sneak in with no one noticing you – I don't want you to become a magnet for criminals."

"Are you scared?"

He read the challenge in her face as he felt his own anger rising. "I go there all the time. You have no idea what it's like – you could get mugged and how am I going to hold off all the thugs in Falaga on my own?"

"I don't care. I'm not afraid of dirt, and I never thought I was going to be 'safe' in Bangita anyway. Come on, let's go! Please!"

He found he was helpless to deny the pleading in her face. Wondering what they were getting into and regretting that he hadn't simply taken her to the tourist attractions in the first place, he turned the key and the motor roared back to life. "Okay, we'll go. Mama Deem, here we come. If we survive the muggers and murderers of Falaga, that is."

They drove across the city through steadily worsening neighborhoods, until they left the paved roads behind, and with them any resemblance to civilization that was recognizable to her. And of course Ben was right: Annie had no idea that anyone could live in a place so filthy, so overwhelmed with horrible smells of rotting garbage, putrefying meat, human and animal waste. They drove slowly down rutted dirt roads, past what seemed like acres of wood, cardboard, plastic, and metal pieces, until Annie saw that there were people moving in and out of doorways among all the pieces, and she realized that she was looking at people's homes: a warren of tiny shacks built of any available material, backed up against each other in a precarious balancing act. There were a few brick and concrete buildings in amongst the shacks, and the shacks leaned against them for support and shelter and almost overwhelmed them. People were everywhere, walking, or riding ramshackle bicycles, and skinny dogs nosed at piles of garbage, their ribs and hip bones showing clearly through their dull and matted coats. They passed dusty grey donkeys pulling rickety wooden carts piled high with wilted produce, or cardboard boxes tied in crazy Dr. Seuss towers, or great mountains of plastic milk jugs tied together by the handles. Once she saw a cart made from the sawn-off load box of an old pickup truck, pulled by two donkeys.

Finally they came to a building that looked as if it might have been a small factory or warehouse. Ben pulled up outside a rollup door and honked the horn. A face appeared at a window and he waved. The face grinned and disappeared, and soon the door began to inch upward. Ben drove the Jeep through the door and into a paved yard, and the small person at the door began to roll the door down again, pulling on the chain hand over hand, at the same time shooing away a skinny cur that tried to put its nose inside. Ben and Annie climbed out of the Jeep and as the child at the door came over to greet them, Annie realized first that she was a girl, and next that her beautiful smiling face topped a body crippled and deformed by accident or disease, so that she moved with a hobbling, twisting gait. Still she flung herself at Ben with abandon and as he hugged her he lifted her and swung her around so that her laughter echoed around the courtyard. He put her down and turned to Annie.

"Annie, this is Marteya. Marteya, I want you to meet my friend Annie."

Marteya's bright eyes took in Annie's appearance and then looked at Ben. Something in his face met her approval and she turned and held out her little hand to Annie. "Welcome to Shamah-abeh," she said, and Annie saw that she was not a child, but a young woman. Her crippling deformity and poor nutrition had combined to stunt her growth, and she was no bigger than an average ten-year-old in the US.

"Thank you," murmured Annie, overwhelmed by the onslaught on her mind and senses.

"Come inside! Mama Deem will be pleased to see you – on a Saturday, Ben! What a special occasion!" Her happy laughter pealed out again as Marteya led the way into the building. As they walked across the courtyard Annie noticed that it was paved with pieces of broken bricks, concrete pavers, and ordinary stones in intricate patterns, and packed in with dirt instead of grout or concrete. She could not help admiring both the artistry and the thriftiness of the work. She saw that there were raised planting beds against the wall on the opposite side of the courtyard, and she thought she recognized tomatoes and other vegetables growing there.

Inside, it was clear there was little money to be had, but the same level of care Annie had seen outside was visible here. There were bookshelves artfully constructed from bricks and scraps of wood and filled with battered books. Children's artwork crayoned on random pieces of scrap paper hung on the walls, and the walls themselves and the simple furniture were painted in a bright jumble of color that created a feeling of happy cheer in absolute contrast to the grey and brown despair of the streets outside. Sunlight streamed through small windows set high up in the walls. Children of all ages and sizes played on the floor, where vinyl tiles and strips in multiple colors and designs made patterns and designs. Women were cleaning up after a meal in an area that was set up as a kitchen and dining area: shelves, countertops, tables and benches were constructed from concrete blocks and wooden planks, all happily splashed with colorful paint. In one corner stood a battered piano, and in another a wrinkled old woman sat in a rocking chair, feeding a small baby with a bottle of milk. Marteya led Ben and Annie over to her.

"Mama Deem, look who has come to see you!" she announced happily. Mama Deem looked up at Ben and her face wrinkled even more as she smiled at him. "And this is Annie, his new girlfriend," Marteya added, her eyes twinkling mischievously as she turned to them. They glanced at each other, startled, and Annie found herself blushing even as she read the question in his smiling eyes. She looked away at the old woman, forcing herself to concentrate and ignore her confused feelings.

"Hello, Mama, it is very good to meet you," she said, reaching out to take the gnarled old hand and finding instead that the baby's bottle was being placed in her own. Mama Deem patted the arm of a second rocking chair next to hers, and handed the baby to her so that she could finish feeding it. Annie sat. Settling the baby in the crook of her arm, she watched it suck eagerly at the milk until it was gone. She lifted the little head to her shoulder and patted its back till it burped loudly, and then its little bright eyes grew droopy and it went to sleep in her arms as she rocked. Conversation flowed around them and the children chattered and played in the big room. Ben had been engulfed by a wave of happy children and he sat with them on the floor. Annie watched them as they played, but she did not recognize any of the children she had seen at the airport, and her heart grew heavy as she thought about what might have happened to them.

Finally Ben stood up. "You look so comfortable there," he said, smiling down at her.

"I am comfortable," she replied, and smiled in return. "This baby is an angel."

Marteya gently took the sleeping baby from her. "Yes, she is an angel who has wet your skirt," she observed.

They all looked at the damp patch on the front of Annie's denim skirt, and looked a little anxiously at her face to see her reaction; their relief was palpable when she burst out laughing. "Falaga has done its worst!" she said, and they laughed with her.

Back in the car, they were quiet as Ben negotiated the rutted and crowded streets of Falaga. They drove across town to an area that seemed more familiar to Annie and stopped outside a small restaurant.

"I had planned to bring you here for lunch," said Ben, "But if you need to just go home and change, that's okay."

"Thanks, but I'm fine – my skirt is quite dry now and you can hardly see the mark. And anyway, I'm hungry for more of that great food we had the other day."

They went inside and ordered salads and chicken curry. As they waited for the food, she said to him, "Tell me more about Mama Deem and the orphan house. What did Marteya call it?"

"They call it *Shamah-Abeh*. It means endless good health, longevity, that kind of idea. It's a kind of in-your-face against Mama Deem's name – they call her *Ahgadeem-Abeh*, which means the one who mourns ceaselessly. She lost all her own children and her husband, but one day she just decided she wasn't going to sit and mourn forever, so she got up and did something to help others who were worse off than she was. She has people from different church groups and charities that help her with supplies and volunteer hours and so on."

"What's Marteya's connection with Shamah?"

"Marteya was one of Mama Deem's first babies. She was hit by a car and her parents couldn't afford to take her to the hospital, so they left her in a box on Mama Deem's doorstep. She was about three then. I think she's about eighteen now."

"Isn't there something they could do for her?"

"They say there is surgery that could help her a lot, but of course they can't afford to do it." They were quiet as they thought about the frustrating reality of a life like Marteya's.

"What's with all the different colors of paint on everything?" Annie asked after a while.

He laughed. "There's a big paint factory here in BC, and they sometimes give away the odd bits of paint that are left over from their color experiments. You just have to take what you can get, so that's what they did! Same goes for the vinyl on the floor; it's just off-cuts and leftovers, whatever they could get for free. Looks fun though, doesn't it?"

Annie had to agree, though images flashed through her mind of perfectly color-coordinated church nurseries and daycare centers where she had worked as a teenager, and the health care and safety standards they had worked so hard to uphold, and she shook her head to clear it as her mind tried to process what she was seeing and learning.

"You said that you go there Sundays, right? Will you be going tomorrow?" she asked.

"Sure we will. Do you want to come?" he offered eagerly, and it was agreed, as steaming fragrant food was placed on the table and they began to eat.

The next afternoon at Shamah-Abeh, Annie found the opportunity to talk with Mama Deem as Ben and the rest of the church group led the children in a round of games, singing, and stories. They spoke of the children, and Mama Deem knew each one, and told their stories with loving simplicity. Marteya brought the little baby to Annie to feed again, and she fed her and rocked her to sleep, as before.

"This one, coming here, this is Bheta. His mother had AIDS. There was no one left to care for him, so when the mother knew her time was near, she came here and put the baby in the nest and so we have him now." A tiny boy toddled over to Mama Deem's side, and she took him on her lap and rocked him as she spoke.

"What is the nest?" asked Annie.

"Marteya can show you. It is a place in the wall of our home here, where anybody who cannot care for their child may put their child without fear, and the child will be cared for. We do not just feed the children, but we love them also. It is necessary to be loved, and not only to be fed," said the old woman, rocking gently in her chair and nodding her head thoughtfully as she spoke. The little boy, Bheta, sucked his thumb and lay quietly in her arms, and she smiled lovingly down at him.

"That one, there, the tall one, that is Abeya. Her mother disappeared, and the neighbor got tired of watching her, so she put her out with the garbage. Luckily the driver of the garbage truck knows where we are, and he brought her to us. She is a bright girl, good at her lessons. She will go far."

"Mama, can I ask you a question?" The old woman nodded, and her bright eyes shone in her wrinkled face. "What made you do this? Take in all these children?"

The old woman rocked a little longer in silence, and gazed at the happy faces of the children as they sang. When she spoke, her voice was soft and Annie had to lean a little closer to hear her. "I looked at the children of the streets, here in Bangita City," she said, "and I thought of the children I had lost, and the tears I had shed for my lost ones, and I knew their pain. The Lord Jesus says, if you take care of the little ones, you take care of him, and if you give your life away, you will receive it back again. Other people, they said to me, 'You are old. Your soul is weary with too much weeping. Why then do you take all these children, and accept many more tears for your soul? – for these children will surely also die.' And I said to them, 'What do you know of my soul?' "

They sat in companionable silence, watching the children, until it was time to leave. Marteya came to take the sleeping baby from Annie's arms.

"We are calling her Annie, after you," she said, "because yesterday was her first day here, and she slept in your lap. We found her in the nest just before you arrived."

"I am honored – thank you! Mama said you could show me the

nest?" Annie found her emotions in turmoil as she followed the younger girl to a quiet hallway, where a large sturdy wire cage protruded out of the wall. Inside there was a soft mattress pad. Access to the box was via a padlocked door on the inside, but on the outside there was a sliding metal panel that anyone could open.

"We have to keep it locked or burglars could get inside the building," explained Marteya, "but the other side is easily opened. Then a bell rings in the big room so we know if someone has put a baby in here. We have an arrangement with the authorities and we simply register the child as part of the Shamah-abeh family."

Email: July

Charlie, I wish you could be here to see everything I'm seeing... I don't know where to start. Well, there is this very nice guy I've met...! His name is Ben Grant and he has taken me to a few places around town, one of them an orphanage – they had a little baby come in there just before we visited and they have named her Annie, after me... crazy and cool. There is a girl there called Marteya, who needs surgery but can't afford it. There are so many needs and no way to even start meeting them! But the lady who runs the orphanage just figured she could do something, even if it's not much, or not enough. So even though my little effort may be pathetic, I should go ahead and do it anyway-!?! Anyway we go there as often as we can, just to help hold and feed the babies. I really like Marteya; even though she has such a severe handicap, she has such faith and always seems so happy to be alive.

Meeting so many new people and situations at once is overwhelming. They told me to expect that; they call it culture fatigue, as opposed to culture shock. You expect some of the major differences, you know the food will be strange and the language etc. It's just that you get tired of always having to think so hard about everything, what you're saying and how to say it and trying to remember everything that's different. Like putting the toilet paper into the trash instead of flushing it... I was so surprised about that, and that it doesn't smell. You're just in the habit of doing things one way and then EVERYthing is different, the most basic stuff. Some people handle it like Mrs. Palmer does: she keeps her house as if she were in the States. Every time she goes 'home' she brings back a ton of food and stuff for her home, so that it instantly transports you right back home. She doesn't like to eat Bangese food; she only ever cooks American-style food, though she's always saying how cheap the food is here. When there are starving people everywhere. THEY don't think the food is cheap, the Bangese, I mean. That seems so strange to me. Serious cognitive dissonance. But if you have dollars then it does seem cheap when you do the conversion.

Anyway I will quit babbling now, hope to hear from you soon,
Annie

Part III: Journeys

The hunter paused near the edge of the water, knowing
What danger lurked in the shadows. With longing
He thought of the family tribe lost, decimated by a disease
That caught them silently, unprepared. One by one
They fell, till only he and one woman were left.
Strong she had been, and a hard worker. Though young,
She had satisfied him in ways his older woman had not.
The image of her face swam unbidden to his mind, the gleam
Of her deep eyes, the curve of her cheek. His skin
Tingled with the memory of the smoothness of her body,
The sweet line of hip and thigh. He felt the blood move in his loins.

The weight of their son, feather light as he was,
Hung as a stone around his neck, and he moved ahead
Into the open, to cross the water. Survival. For both.
Food, water, warmth. A woman to feed the small one?
He was the hunter.

"It is impossible! You cannot allow that girl to go out there to live with those – those – wild people. Life here in the city is barely tolerable. How can you even be *thinking* about it?" Ada could feel her face burning with the blood of her passionate emotion. How could he be so blind about this? Really, men just don't *think*. "Can't you see that allowing one girl to be so vulnerable makes all women vulnerable? What happens if something goes wrong – what do you think it will do to *your* mission?"

"We are not keeping her in town and that's final!" Palmer glared at his wife. "Missionaries cannot live in their own cultural bubble and expect to make any impact on the people of the country they're in!"

"I'm not talking about a bubble! She can teach school here in town. She can go up there every once in a while. Just don't expect her to *live* there! Do you have any idea what kind of conditions she will be living under?"

"I know exactly what the conditions are – I have actually been there myself. I would live there myself if…" His voice trailed off as he saw the look on her face. She in turn saw his anger fade and resignation take its place, and she watched him turn from her. He sat down suddenly, as if the bones had gone out of his legs, and his entire body sagged with defeat. His head dropped into his hands, and his shoulders heaved with dry sobs. She was shaken and a little afraid. This man was a fighter by nature, a doer, an achiever. Her world trembled and moved into realms unknown. She sank to her knees beside him, and reached out a tentative hand to touch him. She began to stroke his arm and croon, *honey, honey, don't cry, please honey,* as she struggled with her own fear. Slowly his sobs died away, and he sat slumped in the chair. She stroked his arm and looked around at her pretty kitchen and wondered suddenly at the incongruity, and felt her world tilt at another crazy angle.

"I am so tired," he whispered. "Tired of fighting. I fight with people in the government here, with people in the church at home, with the heat and disease and dirt and ignorance - and now with you too. I'm sorry, honey, I just need…" His voice trailed off again.

"What do you need?" she asked awkwardly.

He looked up at her through eyes bleak with despair. "I need you … to help me, not to keep on going against everything I do."

"But – I don't really… I mean…" She stopped, uncertain.

"What do you mean?"

"You're undermining me, Ada. The way you talk to that girl, you make her feel like she'll be wasting her time. You don't understand how valuable she is, what she could achieve out there. And then there's the Grant boy. You're getting in between them and I don't understand why."

He saw a spark of anger in her eyes and as her defenses rose against him, and he sensed her stiffen and withdraw. Her voice was cold.

"I'm just trying to help. You know how people feel about that family; you know how people feel about any of these mixed-up families here. It just doesn't seem right to let her get involved with him. I'm sure her family wouldn't approve." Her head came up and she withdrew her hand, turning from him.

He knew the gesture for what it was, and he in his turn withdrew into himself. With effort he straightened up and stood. "I have work to do at the office," he said, and left the room.

She sat still at the table, caught between her need for him and her need to be right. Yielding to him meant yielding all that was familiar and dear to her, the security of the world-within-a-world that she had created for herself, and her fear of the unknown was too great. She listened to the sounds he made, knowing what each one meant: picking up briefcase and keys, shuffling through papers in the hallway, and finally the metallic click of the latch as he closed the front door softly behind him. Even after she heard his car drive away she sat still in the quiet house, the ticking of the kitchen clock loud in her ears, and her eyes were filled with doubt and insecurity, and slow, fat tears.

She heard a car stop outside and dashed the tears from her face. She went to the window to see who was out there. *I'm not paranoid,* she told herself, *just careful. It's getting late and you need to know what's happening in your neighborhood. People are robbed and mugged all the time in this crazy country.* She stood behind the drape so that she could not be seen from the street, and saw Ben Grant's jeep. She watched as Annie and Ben talked for a while, then her heart sank as she saw Ben lean over and kiss Annie, who certainly didn't seem to mind. *Well, if she is that sort of girl, she is not the sort we want setting the example for our teenagers,* thought Ada Palmer. *What should I do now?*

Just then, the phone rang, and when she answered, she found

exactly the sort of situation that she dreaded.

"Hello, Ada? This is Charlotte! How are you doing? It was so good to see you this morning. Didn't you think it was a lovely service? I know you have to visit all the churches but it must be so nice for you to be at First Church." Charlotte: expatriate, fussy and overbearing, always hovering over her children anxiously.

"Hello Charlotte! Oh yes, I thought that was an excellent sermon, and I just loved the choir special," Ada replied warily.

"That new missionary girl you have there certainly seems to be getting involved. My Jenny was out at Shamah-abeh today with the Sunday school group, and she says they have named one of the babies after Annie because she went out there with Ben Grant and was the first to feed the baby. Isn't that sweet?"

"Oh, that is sweet! I hadn't heard about a new baby. I guess they get them all the time." Ada's mind raced as she tried to anticipate where this might be going.

"Yes, I suppose so," said Charlotte. She seemed to hesitate, and her voice took on a confidential tone. "Are you sure she should be running around town with Ben? Apparently she goes out to Falaga with him all the time, and they've been seen all over town together too. You know, we just don't want to be encouraging our girls to hang out with those wild Grant boys. Do you think she knows anything about him?"

"Well, I tried to tell her about him," Ada replied carefully. "But you know how these girls can be when they're fresh out of college and haven't been away from the States much. Still, I'm sure it will be okay. You know she's not staying here in town, don't you?"

"No, I hadn't realized that. Where will she be going?"

"She will be starting a school up in the jungle. There's this village up there they discovered when they started logging in that area. Quite fascinating, really," and Ada found herself enthusiastically endorsing her husband's plan to send Annie far, far away.

Email: August

Hey big bro!

Well I am finally going to start the school in the village. There is a big controversy about that, because I'm a woman and that doesn't fit in with the cultural norms. I am so not used to a place where you can actually say that, and not hire someone because of their gender. I was really mad, but the Palmers calmed me down and said I had better learn to keep my temper. Apparently, women have to know their place around here. I'm still in a bit of shock over that and not sure how to handle it. I didn't even think I was into women's lib!

Anyway, Mr. Palmer is for my going but Mrs. Palmer thinks it's a terrible idea. I think he is going to just do it no matter what anyone thinks! I find that I misjudged him so much at first. He seemed so distant and cold, but I think he has a huge passion to see things change for the people here and he is continually frustrated by everyone, even the people he wants to help.

I can't wait. For the past six weeks I've been helping out at the mission offices downtown. There's always a mountain of paperwork to get caught up on, so I've been setting up filing systems and indexing the library and that kind of thing. I could have done office work back home and gotten paid for it too. I know this helps the missions too but it's hard for me to see that when it's not what I signed up for.

Anyway, it turns out that having my suitcase stolen has ended up being a good thing, or I wouldn't have met Ben. Plus, staying in the city has given me a chance to get to know the country a bit. Yes, and Ben too! He often goes up into the mountains and forest areas because of his job, so I went with him the other day. I am falling in love with this country. It's so beautiful! It seems really wild, but you don't see many animals at all. The people are hungry and they eat anything they can catch so I guess the animals know to stay away from anywhere the people are. Poaching is a huge problem, even in the protected areas. I guess, even if you're really committed to conservation, the idea that someone will pay a colossal amount of money for the skin of a particular animal could be a huge temptation. So if you haven't a foggy clue what conservation is, what's going to stop you? Most people are just trying to survive. And conserve their own families?

Anyway, after I leave here, I won't be able to email any more, but I will write you a long letter every month. I think the plan is to have me back here for Christmas, so I will try to call you then too.

Much love,
Annie

Katu! Katu!

The child heard keenly amidst the general jabber and clatter his mother's voice, calling, always calling. He knew he was the pride of her life but took delight in independence, in pretending the swagger of nonchalance he admired in the men who said they needed not these noisy women, but kept them as one keeps a dog. Yet a part of his mind wondered how they would manage without the clever hands of his mother as she prepared the meat the men brought her, or the green things she found in the forest or dug from her garden. He loved the smell of her, and remembered even the taste of her sweet milk until the little usurper had come.

The usurper was four years old now, and his rival for his mother's attention. She slept in his mother's hut; she helped with the chores and learned the skills of cooking and growing things. He hated her. He loved her, with passionate fascination and anger that he should do so. At nine years old, he had a sow and her piglets to watch. He could not be forever at the knees of his mother but must take his place as a man among the men of his tribe.

His father's other sons took care of the family's goats. Their mother was dead. The cat-god had taken her. *What does it feel like when the cat-god takes you?* he had wondered, when his half brothers had described in gory detail the body of their mother brought in for burial. The people of the village prayed that the cat-god would be satisfied with her sacrifice, and indeed it had left them alone a long time now.

Katu! Katu!

He sauntered over and greeted her with insolence. She had a little sweet cake for him, and she crooned over him as he ate it, plucking at his hair to clean and straighten it. He was pleased and enjoyed the attention, sidling his eyes to where he saw the girl-child, his sister Tulah, pulling weeds in the vegetable plot. He saw her little hand wipe sweat from her face and leave there a streak of the red clay she worked with. It turned his heart within him, and he pushed his mother aside roughly and strode off, shouting, *Enough, woman! There is work to be done!* He did not turn to see the yearning in her eyes, the hunger for affection, but hardened his heart against the women, while his mother turned her sharp pain to anger against the little one, and cuffed and abused her for being born female, and a victim.

The Land Rover arrived in a cloud of noise, with the clashing of gears and roaring of the straining motor. They had heard it coming from several miles away down the trail to the logging road. The silence that descended after the motor died seemed deafening. Katu saw that his people had turned from what they were doing and stood watching as two people climbed out of the vehicle. He recognized the man Palmer, the American who had promised them a school and a clinic. The missionary seemed to have access to government departments and other mysteries that got in the way of progress for the village. Katu had often heard the men talk about it around the fire in the men's hut at night. The other person was a woman, but like no other woman he had ever seen. Her skin was pale like the man's, and her hair was short and colored like the white-gold gleam of dried grass stalks. She was covered with white clothing, as white as the shining clouds in the sky above the clearing, and she wore clothes for her feet like the missionary man. She also had on the small shining eye-shields that he wore. They were dark so that you could not see the eyes or read the expression in them. Katu hung back in the shadows, where he could watch and not easily be seen. His pig was safe in her thorn-brush shelter. He slipped away towards the meeting hut.

Some men of the village approached and greeted the visitors. "Good day, Mr. Palmer. Are you well? And your family - they are well too?"

"Good day to you. Yes, thank you, we are well. Here is the teacher I told you would come for the children's school. Is the school hut ready for her?"

The men shuffled their feet and looked around. Some cleared their throats. They were becoming accustomed to the abruptness of the white foreigner's manner, but even so, sometimes his rudeness amazed them.

"Would you and the young lady care to sit down and have some tea?" asked one of the elders gently, to remind him of the usual custom.

"Thank you. That would be pleasant. I have some time, but I must get back to the city before dark."

They moved slowly towards the large square hut, the village's meeting hut. It was also the men's sleeping hut, and no woman was permitted to enter there. Even the sweeping and the setting of the fire was done by boys. The men stopped and there was some whispered conversation. Katu watched as one of the younger men called over two boys who stood nearby. One of them ran off to where the women worked the vegetable gardens, while the other went into the large hut and came out with a small and elaborately carved stool. This he placed carefully in the shade of a great spreading tree close by. One of the men invited the woman to sit down on the stool, and they squatted in a semicircle around her after much polite jockeying so as to get Palmer next to her and themselves as far from her as possible. There was stilted and polite conversation about the weather, inquiries as to their health and that of their families, and discussions about the poor hunting and poorer crops that season.

Two young women brought large, flat baskets on their heads and began to serve the visitors and the men. One of the young women brought the foreign woman a carved wooden cup and the other poured into it steaming, fragrant tea. They offered her small sweet cakes. Katu watched as she ate and drank. She stared around her boldly, even looking at the men as they spoke. It seemed to him that she had the confident manner of the witch woman who came occasionally to the village. What kind of woman was this?

Katu saw her face turn red. He was amazed and fascinated as he watched the red fade again from her cheeks. How did she do that? He listened and realized that this was the long-awaited teacher. Were they insane? How could they expect men to learn from a woman? Perhaps they would keep her to teach the female children, but what teaching would be necessary for females that their mothers could not teach them? Women did not go to the city or talk to strangers. What need would they have for the white people's teaching? He felt uneasy and insecure.

The men sent for two young women, who went to the Land Rover and unloaded some large bags. Palmer made strange babbling sounds, and the woman replied in the same way. Each took the right hand of the other and shook it in a strange ritual, then the man got into the vehicle and drove away and she hurried after the girls who had her bags. She tried to get some of her baggage from them, but they resisted her efforts. Finally one of them reluctantly yielded a small bag. Did she not trust them? They were the headman's daughters! Katu followed them at a distance between huts, cooking fires, and animal shelters to a small hut near the edge of the clearing, barely a hundred feet from the nearest trees. The immense towering gloom of the forest stood as a wall around the cheerful bustle of the clearing. It was good, thought Katu, that they had put her so far from the men's hut, or who knew what sort of witchcraft she might perform? He laughed silently to himself. That was the hut of his half-brothers' mother, who had been taken by the cat. Perhaps her witchcraft would not be strong enough to overcome the cat, and she would be taken too. He slipped away to find his friend Batah, to share the joke with him.

Later that evening as they drowsed on their mats in the gloom of the great hut, the boys listened as the men discussed the situation in low tones. It was very difficult, for always before a woman had a man to watch over her, father or husband or brother, and each man had his own woman or women to protect and provide for. In this way children were also protected and nurtured, and the social fabric of the clan could be preserved. A single woman, unprotected, might upset the delicate balance of their community life. The men grunted and sighed, murmured and debated. The rumble of their voices lulled the boys to sleep long before they could reach any comfortable solution. They would simply have to wait out the time until she herself would see the impossibility of her remaining there, and leave of her own accord.

Journal Entry: September

I guess it's just one of those times when I wonder what I am doing here. Wherever I am, I feel like I don't fit in. Wanting to become a missionary made me so different from my friends at college, but coming to Bangita was just another step into weirdness. I feel that I am getting nowhere with these people. Teaching them about stuff like reading and writing seemed such a good idea until I came here and saw how much they know about stuff that I am ignorant about. Anyway, at least I know about hygiene and I've been able to help with some little things, like getting splinters out and cleaning up infected grazes. Yesterday Takatu's little girl got some kind of bug in her ear and we got it out with my tweezers – such a simple little item, yet so useful. Anyway I'm glad I had them. And I am learning about the way to survive here, about the food in the jungle and that sort of thing. I have also started a garden and my vegetables look good. I just seem to spend all day taking care of food issues – hauling water, picking bugs off plants, watering plants, looking for plants in the jungle, cooking things and eating them... Maslow and his hierarchy of needs make a lot more sense when you're living it out than it does in college when it's only a theory!!!

Anyway, God, I trust that you know why I am here, because it doesn't make a lot of sense to me.

Letter: September-?

Dear Charlie,

I can't believe I am really here. As you can see, I am not even sure of the date right now. I will have to get a calendar so I can cross off the days; I didn't even think of that. This is nothing like what I expected - I guess I thought there would be a real house for me to live in. But I have a thatched hut in the middle of the jungle. I have asked myself why I came here over and over again. I wouldn't tell anyone but you what I am feeling, because I just know they would give me a hundred scripture verses to read and tell me all about what God has called me to do etc. I know all that and I do truly believe that God has a plan here for me, but what it is I have no way of knowing right now. I have to tell someone how I feel or I'll go crazy. Please don't say anything to Aunt Ginny. I know she will only worry.

There is no furniture in my hut, as we understand furniture, just a grass mat on the floor and a water container made from a gourd. No running water. I brought a bowl and bucket that I can bathe in or wash my clothes. I'd give a lot for a hot shower and a Laundromat! My hair doesn't wash properly in the cold water. The suitcase that was stolen at the airport had all my breakables in it, so all my creams and shampoos went and I had to buy stuff in town when I first arrived, and somehow it just doesn't seem the same. My hairdryer was in it too - and my CD player, CDs, tapes - what a joke!! What was I thinking of? Electricity? What's that?

The people look after me well enough. They brought me food and water every day until I started learning how things worked; now I help some when I can. And the food is okay, though a hamburger never sounded as good as it does now. I just feel so useless! They will hardly talk to me. I walk around in the mornings and say hello to people, and they kinda smile and carry on with whatever they're doing. I want to help the women with their cooking and stuff, but they don't want me to do anything. It's like they're offended or something. You know, like, don't I think they can do it properly? The men don't talk to women except to give orders, or they talk to their wives privately when they visit them in the women's huts. The women work so hard all the time in their gardens, and gathering roots and things in the forest, and cooking and minding babies. If they start talking to me one of the men *will call them and they have to go do something for him. The boys are as bad as the men and just ignore me. The little girls help their mothers. Some of the men go out hunting in the forest but others just sit around - I'm not sure what they're supposed to be doing.*

So basically I can't do what I came here to do, which is teach. They were expecting a man to come, to teach the boys, and I definitely can't do that. They reckon girls don't need to read or write. I think they just want me to leave but are too polite to say so, and will just freeze me out until I choose to go. To tell the truth, I almost did. It just seemed impossible at first. At home we are just so spoiled with hot showers every day and any kind of food we want, just go to the supermarket and buy anything, no matter how exotic or out-of-season it is. Or even better, go to a restaurant and have someone else cook it and serve it and clean up afterwards. And then – beds! Pillow-tops and hand-tied springs and dial-your-own-comfort-level! All I have is a straw mat on the ground and some blankets I brought with me, much too hot to sleep under of course, but they help to pad the ground a little. And no privacy, really; I mean, the walls of my hut are made of thatch so there are little gaps in it everywhere that my white skin shines through... Please pray for me that I will have some kind of breakthrough with someone! At least I have plenty of time to pray, read the Word, and practice the guitar! I have been trying to compose some little songs in Bangese and I sit outside my hut after the evening meal and sing. Some of the children listen, though they don't come near. It's as though they're afraid of me.

There are a few bright spots in my life! Mr. Palmer's visits are definitely one of them, since he brings the mail and stuff I need from the stores. Also he speaks English!!! Though he only comes once a month. Then there is Ben Grant (I told you about him) who is a conservation official and does a regular trip out to this area, so he comes out here to Kinta village, now that I am here. His father is American and Mrs. Grant is Bangese. I heard from Mrs. Palmer that some people don't approve of them very much - on both sides of the cultural divide. I guess people are the same all over the world. So at least there are two people here that I can talk to sometimes! Actually three: the woman who looks after me. Her name is Takatu, because she has a boy called Katu (who won't talk to me because he is way too grown up. He's about nine years old!). She also has a cute little girl of about four who actually smiled at me this morning! Well, in a shy sort of way from behind her mother's skirts. I am hoping that I will be able to convince Takatu to teach me how to do the work they do. Maybe

49

that way I can befriend the women and some of the kids.

Well, I do feel better for having unloaded some of that. Thanks! That's what brothers are for, right? I'll finish off now because I'm expecting Mr. Palmer today and he'll take the mail out for me. And in case you were wondering, a letter would be WONDERFUL.

Much love,
Annie

PS. How selfish I am! I haven't even asked how med school is going! I can't believe you're almost done! Please let me know the names of all the girls who are swooning into your arms so I can write and tell them what you're REALLY like!!! (kidding!!)

Journal Entry: It's Sunday

It's Sunday and doesn't feel much like it. When I first came I didn't know what to do about Sunday, but a few weeks ago I finally decided that if I didn't celebrate the Lord's day I would lose something too precious, even if I must do it alone. How I miss church! How guilty I feel for all the times I groaned about getting up on a Sunday morning for services and Sunday school! First Thessalonians says I must rejoice always, pray constantly, and give thanks in ALL circumstances!! How far short I fall! So now Sundays are my day for resting in the Lord, singing hymns, and reading the Bible aloud, as loud as I can. It gives me good practice in reading Bangese. Mr. Palmer says that next year he will come and lead a service on a Sunday once a month. He seems to think I am making good progress, though at what I can't imagine. No, I must give thanks. Not complain. So here goes.

- *Thank you God, for my hut. It keeps out the rain surprisingly well. And is beautifully crafted. I don't know who made it but they did a good job.*
- *Thank you, God, for my sleeping mat. Thank you for helping me get used to it, to sleeping on the ground. Thank you for the Mexican blankets I brought with me - they are so practical - they don't show the dirt!*
- *Thank you for my Bible and my guitar and my songbooks and my notebooks. Thank you for my wash bowl and towels. Thank you for the Palmers and the way they support me.*
- *Must I thank you for the bugs too? Okay, thank you for the skeeters and all the horrible creepy things. I can see no earthly use for them but I trust you!!*
- *Lord Jesus, thank you most of all for coming to earth from heaven. For the first time in my life I begin to appreciate what it must have been like for you to go to live in a Middle Eastern peasant village of two thousand years ago. The dirt, the flies, the what-on-earth-is-this food, the suspicion, the cold rejection of the outsider! Dear God, forgive me for grumbling, for taking electronic-age American life for granted. If I miss my family and my church fellowship so much, how much harder it must have been for you to miss the beauty and close fellowship of Heaven! Thank you for doing it for us. And thank you for giving me the privilege of doing this for you.*

Journal Entry: October

What a gift! Today Takatu showed me how to bake the bread we eat here, and she told me that she will take me with her tomorrow when she goes to get herbs. I think it's because I was able to help her little girl, Tulah, when she hurt herself the other day. The little first aid kit I brought was great, though I can see I will need to get more supplies. Just tweezers to get the splinters out, peroxide to clean it all, and some antiseptic cream, and I'm a medicine woman -!

Letter: October

Hey Charlie,

It was so good to get a letter from home – and a parcel of goodies! You are the best brother ever. The candy was perfect - I got to share it with some of the people here - and I love the tee shirt. Thank you, thank you!

I am slowly getting used to this life. It sure is healthy, plenty of fresh air and homegrown vegetables - I have never been so fit in my life! Sleeping on the floor and cold sponge baths are not so bad – at least the cold water is refreshing in this sticky heat. And I just know you have been praying for me, 'cause some good things are happening! That breakthrough I was hoping for has happened with my friend Takatu and her little girl. One day I asked if I could borrow her broom and when I returned it she showed me that she had started to make one for me, so I sat there and she showed me how she was doing it. Then the next day I asked if I could go into the forest with her and she showed me some of the plants they were picking and we were both so happy when I found some! That night when I played my guitar she came with her little girl and sat with me and the next night too, and then she started bringing some of her friends, and pretty soon we were laughing and teaching each other songs and they wanted to try out the guitar. The men are sort of disapproving. I hope they don't give their wives a hard time because of me.

Do you remember that I told you about Ben Grant? He took me with him one day when he went on one of his trips to the logging camps they have here. It's like in the Amazon jungle; everyone wants to cut down the trees. He says it's a real problem here. The loggers are supposed to be licensed and he goes out to check, but a lot of times there's all kinds of bribery going on, and they don't list everything they have cut, or the license is a forgery. It was so interesting going with him and seeing everything. I thought the island would be much smaller - it looks such a little speck on the maps - but it took us hours to get to the camps and back. It was good to take a break from the village but it felt like home when I got back to my little hut. In December I'll be going to town to stay with the Palmers for two weeks. I am looking forward to having a hot shower! ☺

Ben told me a story that was really weird and disturbing - another one NOT to tell Aunt Ginny! Apparently there is a kind of large cat in the jungle here, some sort of tiger or panther, which is endangered and *may not be hunted. Ben says no one has seen one for ages, but they think the people still hunt them. Of course they sell the skins on the black market, not legally, but once in a while a skin turns up. Anyway a few years ago a woman from our village was killed by one of these cats, and so far as anyone knows, that particular one was never caught. There are hunter-gatherer tribes that still live completely in the jungle, not in permanent villages like Kinta. A few months back the loggers found a woman's body in the jungle and it was brought in, and they did a post-mortem and found she had died in childbirth and then been partly eaten by one of these cats. Yes, I know it's gross, and it's also scary, because the jungle is a few yards from my door, and there is only a sort of brush barricade between me and whatever's out there! So the loggers are all armed and ready to shoot at anything. Well I think they do shoot at anything anyway, to supplement their meals and their incomes. I must say it's very sad to be driving along through this lush jungle and then to come out into one of these denuded areas - it looks like the aftermath of war. Makes me sympathize with the "bunny lovers and tree huggers" - what are we doing to our world? Why do we have to have THIS wood - why not some other cheaper fast-growing kind? And of course it comes back to greed, and the love of money that's the root of all evil - even ecological disaster. And it's not as though the loggers or villagers really benefit from it all - their wages are pathetic and that's why they poach and steal and bribe. It's a mess.*

Well brother dearest, thanks again for the letters and prayers - and I shall have to write soon to this poor unfortunate girl Ashley who has been hoodwinked into going on dates with you...!

Love,
Annie

Journal Entry: November

I am so excited! Some of the the women and girls have started coming to sit with me and are learning the songs. They tell me their stories and I tell them mine. I asked them if they would like to come hear me read from the Bible on Sunday and they came. The men don't like it too much but the headman's mother is also Takatu's grandmother (everyone is connected somehow) and she gave him a mouthful the other day when they thought I couldn't hear, about how the women were doing their work and deserved a little bit of entertainment once in a while. So now I'm official. For the women, anyway.

"What're your plans for today, Annie? Is Ben picking you up again today?"

They sat at the breakfast table in Mrs. Palmer's pretty kitchen. Annie felt as if she had been transported home. She was reveling in the luxury of an early morning hot shower, muffins and coffee for breakfast, carpets and tiles beneath her feet. She was wrapped in a thick terry robe, and slowly savored each mouthful.

"Yes ma'am, he's coming at ten." She sipped again. "Oh ma'am, this coffee is so good," she breathed, eyes closed in bliss. She missed the frown that briefly creased the older woman's brow.

Ada Palmer was still concerned about Annie's situation in Kinta village, and even more unhappy about her ongoing friendship with Ben Grant. It was really not right that an American girl should be going around with a Bangese - even if he did have an American father. And those Grant boys were known to be wild, always running off into the jungle or sailing off around the island or something of the sort. And to make matters worse, her husband still could see nothing wrong in the friendship. Men could be so aggravating. It was just as well their only daughter had stayed stateside after she had graduated from college, or it might have been their own daughter mixed up in an unsuitable relationship, and her husband unwilling to see any problem. She sighed and got up to start on the dirty dishes.

Annie jumped up to help, but Ada shooed her away to get dressed.

"And be sure and bring your laundry through, now, and let's get started on it," she called to the girl's retreating back.

"So are you enjoying civilized life in the big city? Not ready to go back to your jungle yet?" Ben stood and looked at her, a happy grin on his face.

Annie laughed. "No way, Jose! This is way too good. Showers, coffee, real beds - actually, the funny thing was, it was really hard for me to get comfortable – the bed seemed much too soft."

"So what would you like to do today? Shopping, the beach, sightseeing? Your wish is my command!" Ben gave a flourishing bow as he opened the car door for her.

"Well, I would like to do some Christmas shopping, and I need to go to the Post Office to mail a gift home to Charlie – but you know, I can leave that for another day. Let's just have fun today!"

"I was hoping you'd say that! Only one quick stop before we start on the fun part – I need to drop something off at my dad's office for my mother. Do you mind?"

"Not at all! Can I come in and meet him?" she asked. She was curious to meet the man who was willing to defy cultural norms for the woman he loved.

Ben looked surprised and pleased. "Of course; I'd love you to meet him."

They drove to an office block in the downtown area. The American flag flew outside and a large colored seal indicated the embassy. They parked in a metered space on the street and entered the lobby. Security cameras. Unsmiling armed guards at the door. Sign-in and ID checks. State your business. Metal detectors. The reality of concern about people's intentions towards the US. Ben took it in stride, since he went there often, and Annie took her cue from him and accepted it as the norm. They rode the elevator to the twentieth floor.

They waited in a small bare ante-room with hard upright chairs, until an aide came in.

"Hello Ben, good to see you," she said, smiling. "Your dad can see you now."

They followed her to a small, well-appointed office with stunning views over the city and the ocean. A tall, good-looking man stood up from behind the desk and came around to greet them.

"Annie, this is my dad, Chris Grant. Dad, this is Annie Robbins, the teacher I told you about."

Annie put out her hand to shake his and gave a little gasp of surprise. "Oh, it's you!" she said, and was overcome with embarrassment, as both men looked at her, puzzled.

"Have we met before?" Chris Grant asked.

"At the airport, the day I arrived here – you carried one of my bags. It was about six months ago, said Annie, blushing.

The man's face cleared and he grinned, and he looked so much like Ben that Annie at once felt more at ease. "I remember you!" he said. "You had so much stuff you would never have been able to get it all into the terminal on your own. How did you manage after that?"

Realization suddenly dawned on his face. "Oh – maybe it's your bag that we have in the storage locker!"

It was Annie's turn to be puzzled. "You have my bag? How can that be? Someone stole it at the airport."

Chris Grant laughed. "The man who picked it up thought I had left it by mistake, and he returned it to me here at the office, hoping for a reward. There was no label on it, so we were unable to trace the owner. We have been holding it in storage until someone claimed it." He bent to the intercom on his desk and gave instructions to the aide to retrieve the suitcase from the storage locker and bring it to the office.

"Well that was an interesting turn of events," said Ben, still looking as if he wasn't sure what had just happened. They all laughed.

"Sit down and have some coffee with me – I have a break in my schedule right now. That doesn't happen often so you'd better take advantage of it." They sat and chatted, comfortable as old friends, and the aide brought Annie's long-lost suitcase and some coffee. Annie watched and listened as Ben and his father interacted with each other, and she felt that this was the sort of relationship she would have liked to have with her parents, if they had survived.

Later, as Ben drove away towards the beach, he noticed that she seemed quiet and thoughtful. "Are you okay?" he asked. "You seem very quiet all of a sudden."

"I was just thinking how much I like your father. Seeing the two of you together made me really miss my parents." He saw that her eyes held unshed tears. Without a word he reached over and took her hand, and held it as they drove on.

They walked for miles along the beach, chatting freely about their lives and hopes and loves and dreams, holding hands, sensing the deepening of tenderness between them. They sat in the shade of coconut palms in a deserted cove and watched the little waves chasing crabs up the beach. He slid his arm around her shoulders and kissed her, and the intensity of their kiss surprised them both, so that they broke away and stared at each other, aware of a new dimension in their lives.

"I guess I should get back," she said. "The Palmers are expecting me for dinner." They walked back through the little waves with their arms around each other, not speaking much, though their silence was electric with communication.

"How was your day today, dear?" Namira Grant looked at her son across the dinner table and felt again the twin emotions of pride and fear that belonged to all her thoughts of her children. He was a fine boy, a son to be proud of, but too often she wondered if she and her husband had done the right thing in bringing mixed-race children into the bigoted world they lived in.

"It was great, thanks, Ma. Nice to take the day off and do some fun stuff. I took Annie to the beach after we visited Dad at the office. She is back from Kinta village for Christmas."

"I still can't believe they sent her to live up there in the jungle! How is she coping? Poor girl! It must have been quite a culture shock for her."

"I don't know for sure, but it seemed like she was doing okay when I went up to the village last month. She has this little hut and it seems to me the women there are teaching her more than she is teaching them." A small smile played around his mouth as he took another mouthful of his mother's excellent cooking, but Namira knew that the sparkle in her son's eyes did not come from his enjoyment of the food. The little stone of fear in her heart grew heavier.

"What is she like, this girl? To look at, I mean?" She tried to ask casually, to mask the tension in her voice.

"She's very pretty, Ma. All blond hair and blue eyes, and looking really good today because she is staying at the Palmers' and enjoying the city life. I like her a lot. She's fun to be with, and just different, you know? From other girls I've met. She seems to really care about stuff." He sat back in his chair and looked at his mother. He saw the emotion she tried to hide and frowned. "What's up, Ma? What are you not telling me? Don't you want me to see her?"

To the consternation of them both, Namira's eyes suddenly filled with tears and she got up from the table and hurried from the room. Ben heard the bedroom door close behind her. Where was Dad when you needed him? How was he going to figure out what was wrong now? He sat for a minute, frowning, but finally shrugged and turned back to his meal. His thoughts turned again to the subject of their discussion, and the smile returned to his face as he saw again the gleam of her hair in the sunlight, and the little dimple in her cheek when she smiled. She really *was* very pretty.

His mother came back into the room, composed, though her eyes were red. "I'm sorry, Ben, I don't know what came over me," she said, sitting down again at the table. She poured herself a cup of coffee from the pot that sat on a little warmer. As she stirred in sugar and cream, she asked with an effort at casualness, "Would you like to have Annie home for dinner one evening? Since it's Christmas? So she can meet your family."

He looked up at her face and read the conflicting emotion there. "I would love that, Ma. Andy will be home too, won't he?"

"Your brother keeps his own schedule, but I think he is planning to be here for about a week. I would love to meet her. It seems that she is important to you," she said gently.

Ben looked at his mother. She was still lovely, though there were lines around her eyes and mouth and silver threads in her silky black hair. She loved her husband, but the years of trying to fit in for his sake had taken their toll. The round of events with high-flying politicians and bigwigs was something she endured without much enjoyment. *Some things are just meant to be. It is a woman's duty to fit in with her husband's idea of things, to just accept it and make it work for them both.* The litany of her mother's teaching was a constant background to Namira's thoughts and decisions. She looked forward to the day when Chris would retire and they would be able to live near Buccaneer Bay and her family and friends there, but she was not sorry that she had chosen life with him. If her son wanted to make a similar choice, she was his mother and she would do whatever was needed to make it easier for him.

"Ma, you're the best," he said to her. "She *is* important to me. I'm just having a hard time admitting it." The look that passed between them told both that they knew and understood why.

That evening, Annie sat on the floor of her bedroom at the Palmers' home, surrounded by the things she had unpacked from her suitcase. In addition to shampoos, cleansers and lotions, hairdryer,

CDs and CD player, she had packed toys, trinkets, and pictures that held special memories for her or that she had thought might be useful for decorating the walls and shelves in her classroom. She shook her head in rueful amusement at her own ignorance. *What on earth am I going to do with all this stuff?* she asked herself. *I don't even have a classroom, and if I did, it wouldn't have walls or furniture...* she thought of how much these items had meant to her as a teenager and in college, and an idea came to her. She got up and went to find Ada Palmer.

A few nights later she sat and counted the cash she had received for her treasures at the sale they had held. The teen girls from the church and the neighborhood had come with their friends and fallen on her things with whoops of delight. She had also sold them about half of all the clothes she had brought, knowing they were no use to her in Kinta. She planned on taking many gifts back with her after the holiday: things like tweezers, hairbrushes and combs, knives, axes, scissors, cooking pots, buckets with lids... her list was long.

"They really like you, Annie," said Ben. They sat in the car on a hill outside town, a popular viewpoint where the lights of Bangita City lay spread out below, gleaming jewels on the velvet night, and the moon silvered the sea.

"I like them too, Ben; you have a wonderful family," she replied, but her voice seemed distant and she stared out over the city with a troubled look on her face, dimly though he could see her in the moonlight. He felt frustrated; everything had gone so well at dinner. His family had been their wonderful best and she – ! He had thought he might burst with love and pride as he watched her interact with them.

"Then what is wrong? Is it me? Annie, I love you. Maybe you think I'm crazy but I do, I love you. Maybe I'm not good enough for you or something, but I want to marry you. I can't believe I'm saying this, but I do want to marry you."

She looked at him with wide eyes. "Oh Ben, I don't know how you can think you wouldn't be good enough for me – you're amazing. I just can't think about us getting so serious right now. How can I, when I need to go back to Kinta?"

"Why do you need to go back there? You told me yourself they don't want you, that you think you're wasting your time there. Maybe if you leave, they can get a man teacher, like they want to. Marry me; I'll take you back there to visit them. You can have a shower every day and still go see them regularly. Come on Annie, be realistic; they're never going to accept you there."

She looked at his passionate face and felt tears well up in her eyes. "I can't, Ben, not yet, I've got to do this. This is a God-thing, and I don't know yet if our relationship is a God-thing."

"I don't know or care if it's a God-thing, I just know I've never felt this way before and I can't imagine life without you. And if God could let me feel this way about you, and not care, but still send you away, then I don't need God in my life."

She cried, the tears spilling out over her cheeks. "You *do* need God, Ben, you do, and if I'm going to come between you and God then it will be better if I'm not in your life."

He leaned his head on the steering wheel and they sat in unhappy silence for what seemed an age, until he started the car and drove her home in silence. When they stopped outside the house, he said, "I mean it, Annie. I will marry you tomorrow if you will have me."

She looked at him sadly, her eyes still full of tears. Leaning over, she kissed him gently, then got out of the car and silently went inside.

"How was dinner?" called Ada Palmer from the living room.

"It was lovely, thank you!" she called back, and she went upstairs and closed the door, and cried many tears into her pillow.

He drove to the beach, and walked there for many hours, till he fell exhausted to the sand, and slept.

The next morning when Annie came down for breakfast, Ada Palmer could barely contain her excitement. "Oh Annie," she said, "I am so sorry, but I can't help being excited – we've been given flights home for Christmas, and we would have to leave the day after tomorrow. It means we can be with Hannah and her babies, and I can't wait, but, honey, it means we won't be here for you! We can arrange for you to stay with Ms Charlotte, or with Pastor Bob and his family, whoever you want. Just say; I know they will have you in a heartbeat."

Annie looked at Ada's excited face, and found acting abilities she never knew she had, as she pretended to be delighted for the Palmers, while her own heavy heart sank even lower at the thought of spending Christmas with strangers. Separated from her brother and aunt by the miles, and now from Ben also, Christmas suddenly seemed empty and meaningless.

"Ma'am, do you think perhaps Mr. Palmer would have time to drive me back to Kinta before you leave? I think I would like to share the Christmas story with my friends there, and I have all sorts of lovely gifts for them. I'm sure that's what I'm meant to do, ma'am, if you think he can manage it."

So after a little argument it was settled, and Annie found herself bouncing on the hard seat of the Land Rover down the rutted jungle pathways less than a week after leaving. Among the heavy stones in her heart was the knowledge that she hadn't been able to speak to Ben before she left. When she had no answer to her phone call, she wrote a hasty note and left it with Ada Palmer, with agonies of doubt and regret, and a little prayer of resignation, half-meant.

January: Cold Meeting

"Yes, I know this is different than what we have done in the past. That is the whole point. The old ways of doing mission work are ineffective and the people are crying out for real help. We have to stop thinking we can come into a situation and impose our cultural norms and values on other people and call that Christianity. People in foreign countries are wise to the ways of the world, they are educated, they have the internet and technology and what they really need to see is a person living out Christ-likeness in their own context. They are tired of missionaries who tell them how to straighten out their countries' problems, yet live in cocoons of their own culture..."

Tom Palmer looked at the rigid faces in front of him and felt the familiar mix of frustration, anger, and despair well up inside. How would he ever explain to these people what he knew about the Bangese he worked with? If he began to talk about the good things of the Bangese culture, the charming and intelligent and hospitable people he knew there, these men would want to withdraw him from his position. Why was it that you could not admire some things about one culture without making people of another culture think that you didn't like *them*? It seemed to him that every culture and people group he had ever encountered had something unique and lovely about it, and that each could learn from the others. Yet how to get them to see these things? The men who comprised this mission review board had all visited some foreign field; some had even been missionaries for years. They were good men, caring and compassionate, but they were of the old school of thought, which felt that 'going native' was a step down; one should always maintain one's own cultural standards no matter where one lived, and wherever possible, impose those standards on the churches and organizations one founded. None of them was able to recognize the cultural colonialism inherent in this way of thinking. Yet they controlled his resources, made the decisions that allowed him to be in Bangita – if they terminated his position, he would have no option but to return home. Without employment there could be no work permit. The only way he could go without them would be via a lengthy process of trying to prove that he was necessary to the Bangese economy, that no native Bangese could do the work he was doing... He had checked it out, spent sleepless nights wondering how he could make this work better. Despair made him want to give up, anger spurred him on. The Bangese thought he was out of touch with their problems and useless to help them. His own wife couldn't understand what he was trying to do.

The men around the table harrumphed and shuffled papers and muttered to one another. Finally the chairman cleared his throat.

"Thank you for coming in, Brother Palmer. We will meet again tomorrow to consider what you have told us. Please come in again on Thursday morning, nine o'clock."

An extended vacation... A less stressful role in ministry... perhaps an associate position in a midsize church... Perhaps you have lost perspective on our church's way of doing things... Come on home for a while and perhaps things will look different...perhaps you just need a rest... Perhaps perhaps perhaps

On Thursday, Tom Palmer drove for many hours trying to drown the sound of the men's voice-over track to his mental slide show of Bangese faces and scenes, but the litany grew louder and the scenes flashed ever more quickly and he drove faster and faster and with greater and greater despair in his heart and didn't even see the red light, or the semi that crushed his little rental car and took his life.

His wife Ada was well taken care of, in a little cottage at a retirement center for missionaries and preachers, with an adequate pension as befitted the wife of a long-serving and faithful missionary, and she never knew. About what happened at the meeting; about the decisions that were made. About the minutes of the meeting that were carefully edited for kindness' sake, so that she could be taken care of. About her husband's despair. About the fact that no one knew that Annie Robbins was still in Kinta Village, and cut off from the outside world.

Journal Entry: January

Even though things back in BC were so awful, it was good that I went back when I did – bringing back all those gifts ended up being such a blessing to the people here in Kinta, even though it was such a mess at first. It gave me a chance to explain the Christmas story. The things I was able to get were just practical little things that make such a difference.

Then I found out that the headman's new wife, Aheyla, whom I had prayed for, is expecting a baby! It's considered a shameful thing in this culture for a woman not to be able to have children – they just don't understand the biology of it all. So that has given me more opportunity to share and pray with the other women. The men actually grunt and nod in greeting now when I pass them.

I gave Aheyla a pair of tweezers, because she admired mine so much when I took some thorns out of her hand last October, and then last week I got one in my shoulder and she took it out for me... she was so proud of herself. I shouldn't lose sight of the good things that happen, even when they seem so small.

Part IV: Adjusting

The great gleaming beetle labored ponderously to
Be free of a twig corral. The child
Breathed deeply, and dark eyes shone with
Fascination. He lifted the beetle, and giggled
As feathered legs walked the empty air.
The hunter squinted against the blue haze
Drifting from the morning fire. He watched his son
Play, and grunted his amusement and satisfaction.
The child showed him his treasure, delight in his eyes. The father
Touched the child, lightly, uncertain still of the
Emotion that was not proper to display,
Aware that others of the group might
Watch, and disapprove, that he should single out
One child for special attention.
Such feminine weakness hindered survival.
A man's mind must be uncluttered of any thought but
Kill or be killed. That was the law by which
Life continued, or ended. Yet this
Feeling he had for the child would not be tamed or stilled.

He surrendered to the immutability of circumstance.
Such were the ways of the gods,
And who could understand or change them?
Thus had his mother taught him, and well so,
Or how could he have survived when all those
Around him - father, mother, brother, sister, wife -
Had not?
Such thoughts occupied his mind at times, but he
Laid them aside when he left the camp, or
It might have been he who had died this morning at dawn,

And not the monkey which a woman was skinning
Even now. He was a good hunter, and they had been
Glad to accept him into their family group, even with the
Liability of the child. The gods had smiled on him; a woman
Had lost a sucking child to a fever and was eager to take the
Baby he brought. So they survived, he and his son. He
Pondered again the fickle favor of the gods, then
Shrugged and brushed aside the thought like the
Humming flies. He stood, and went to his hammock
To sleep, till the waning afternoon would find him
Once more seeking prey.

Journal Entry: Sometime in April?

I have been without any mail delivery or English-speaking company for so long that I am losing track of the passage of time. I'm not sure what has happened, but Mr. Palmer hasn't been back since he left me here in December. I decided I should update my journal more regularly, so that if anything happens to me, at least there will be some kind of record. Not that I want to become paranoid, but maybe I am already.

I'm not sure what the date is anymore; the days seem to blur into one another and it doesn't really seem to matter so much anyway. So I have missed marking off some days here and there and that makes me lose track. I think it's sometime in April. That means that back home everyone is thinking about Easter and chocolate bunnies... Sometimes I really miss it all and other times it seems very foolish to me. Who can imagine "spring" when surrounded by evergreen forests and endless sticky heat?

I haven't seen Ben since December either. That has been the hardest to bear; I miss him so much. I guess I hadn't realized how much I came to depend on his company. I came to love him without even realizing it, but perhaps he is unable to forgive me for choosing to come back here. If he were to ask me again to marry him, I would say yes, and if I could not do that and be here at Kinta, I would choose him anyway. But I haven't been given that second chance. So I pray daily for these feelings to go away. The Lord reminds me that this is what it feels like to love those who do not love you in return: to love Ben, and to have him not speaking to me, and to love these people here at Kinta as I have come to do, and know that they want me to go away. Even though things have opened up between me and the women here, it is far from perfect or even easy. I am and always will be the outsider, missing the jokes and the cultural nuances.

Letter: April?

Dear Charlie,

Even though Mr. Palmer hasn't been here to bring mail for a long time, I feel like I have to write to you just to feel like I am conversing with someone. Each month I write you a letter, and then when he doesn't come I put it away and start another one, but the truth is I have no idea any more what month it is, so I will just write letters regardless, and you will have a whole book's worth to read when you finally get them all.

When I came back at Christmas with all my carefully chosen gifts, I caused complete chaos, because the first person I gave something to was Takatu, and she bragged to someone else, and I had raised her up above her place in the village or something that I still don't get. That first evening when the women didn't come to read or sing with me I didn't realize at first that they were snubbing me, but it gradually dawned on me the next day that they weren't friendly or open like they had been; there wasn't even singing in the fields and a bad feeling hung over everything.

Then, thankfully, one of the headman's many nephews or cousins came to bring me a message. He stood outside my hut in the evening and cleared his throat loudly until I came out. He came to say that his father wished to meet with me – unheard of – but he led me to the main clearing where they had set up the little chair that I sat on the first day I was here, and the old uncle of the headman was sitting there on a bigger chair, and he so gently and carefully explained to me the ways of gifts and property in the village. There is this whole structure of who can have what, and when, and how, that I will never completely understand in a zillion years, and so I not only upset things by being a single female with no male relative to watch over her honor, but now I had upset the whole tribal structure. Then he said that the village council had talked it over and decided that if I wanted to give any more gifts they would send for them and he and the council would consult with the senior wives about who should get what.

I tried to take it calmly. I thanked him and told him I would think about what he had told me. He told me to send a message to the men when I had an answer for them, by giving this little carved piece of wood he gave me to Takatu to give to Katu to give to his father... so complicated. At first I was so mad – why couldn't I give anything I wanted to to anyone I wanted to? – but as I prayed about it, I realized that if I was ever to get close to being accepted here, I would have to do it their way. So I gave the message stick to Takatu, and she gave it to Katu, who gave it to his father, who gave it to the headman. This took days... Then the old uncle sent for me again, and I thanked him again for explaining to me the ways of his people, since they were so different from the ways of my people. I told him I had many useful gifts for the people of the village, and if he would like to send someone for them, I would be glad to let them decide who should have what. I told him that it was a common custom amongst our people to give gifts at this time of the year to honor our God. He said they would have a gift-giving party in three days' time, and he thanked me for wishing to honor his people with gifts, and that it would be a further honor if I were to tell them the story of my people and their custom.

The next evening, after the evening meal, a group of about twenty young people, teenagers and twenty-something's, gathered outside my hut and the girls called to me as they do. When I came out they told me they had come to help me carry my gifts to the gathering place, so in a grand procession, each person carrying something except me (and I had to walk at the back of the line, which is the place of the honored person), we carried the gifts to the gathering place, where they laid them all carefully in the center of the circle. I had metal bowls and pots and buckets, knives, axes, pieces of fabric, scissors, and needles – all sorts of stuff. The council and the senior women were all there, gathered round in the circle, and they looked at me expectantly when everything had been laid out, as if I should make a speech. So I did.

I said that I was honored to be allowed to live with the Kinta people, and to show my gratitude I had brought many gifts for the village. Then the headman said that they were honored to have me among them (liar! – or maybe they are changing their thinking about me too?) and he announced that there would be a party the day after next, and that I would be telling them the story of my people and their custom of giving gifts.

That's when it dawned on me that I was going to have the chance to tell the Christmas story – I was so excited I almost freaked out totally. The next two days everyone was getting food together and getting out their best sarongs, washing their hair – it was prom season in Kinta! At one stage the men called for me again so that I could explain to them the uses of the many strange things I had brought...

I don't know that I did the best job ever of sharing the Christmas story, but I read from Luke in Bangese and then read John 3:16 and explained why Jesus came. The people love stories and so I tried to *make it as dramatic and interesting as I could. It was so much fun. So my awful blunder ended up being this wonderful God-thing. When they gave out the gifts I saw that it was really a good system, as they made it into a kind of prize-giving for the people who had demonstrated kindness and community spirit as well as just the leaders and headman's family. Plus, because it's such an ordered community, people share their things and help each other when there is a hut to build or repair. They are very strict about not stealing or sleeping around and since there are only about three hundred people in the whole village you can't hide anything like that. Also I had to show people over the next few weeks how to use everything, so I got to interact with lots of different people and teach them all kinds of things. They have appointed a young woman to be my chaperone; she is the youngest daughter of the headman and we guard each other's honor when there are men to be taught.*

Charlie, I hope you get to read this. I also hope I get to see you again someday – soon. I have grown to love the Kinta people, and this is my funny little home, but still I miss you and many other things and people. I love and appreciate you and the way you have been such a good brother to me, especially after Mom and Dad died. I can't imagine how it would be if I never saw you again, but in case that happens, just know that I love you very, very much.

Annie.

Journal Entry: Ten Days Later

Wow - the latest development is one I really don't know how to handle. Because I have no family here – no father or brother – and Mr. Palmer and Ben haven't been here in months, the village men are worrying about my single femaleness. One of the men has been giving me the eye and so the other day I asked Takatu who he was and why he kept looking at me like that. She told me that the men had been discussing the matter of my honor as a female, and he had asked the council to think about whether he would be allowed to take me as his third wife. Apparently since I have no male relative for him to discuss it with, I belong to the whole council. I was really mad and scared but I know I have to keep those feelings to myself! I told Takatu that I am betrothed to Ben and that he is raising the money for a wedding and that's why he hasn't been here to see me. God forgive me for the lie. It's more of a stretch of the truth in some ways, but what do I know? Maybe he has met someone else in the meantime. Maybe "the wild Grant boys" earned their reputation by being wild for girls and not just for being risk takers.

I hope that will have bought me some time until Mr. Palmer comes again. Where is he? I am starting to think that Ben is right and I will never be allowed to be a teacher here and that I should just leave. I really want to talk to Mr. Palmer about that and get his wisdom on this, but it's not like I can just walk out of here and walk to Bangita City, or catch the next bus on the corner. Where IS he? I do NOT want to be some stranger's third wife. Help me God.

Part V: Jungle

Few sounds there were, lately, of animal
Movement, of monkey screech or birdcall.
Farther and farther each day the hunters roamed to find
The smallest meal. Men grew morose. Women
Snapped at children, who whined at their emptiness.
Little ones and the old grew listless. The men
Consulted in low tones.

One, new returned, told of a place
Where the forest was dying.
There was vast noise. Men with giant clashing animals
Ripped and ate the trees, loaded them on great
Beasts that roared away on paths wide enough
For ten deer. The animals were afraid and hid.
They would have to follow.
The other men desired to see this thing of which he spoke.
They wondered, and politely doubted, for
Never before had they seen an animal that would eat
Whole trees. Bark, yes, and fruit and leaves -
But how could one invent such a tale?
Their brother insisted it was so; he could take them.
Thus was it decided to go, to see, and then
To follow the animals by which they lived.

Shadows among shadows, they stood among trees
And saw a wounded place where no trees grew,
A great open place where the sky looked down
At the floor of the forest.
They saw men sleeping, and the giant
Beasts of which their brother spoke.

The earth was torn; leaves and roots lay dead
As after the great windstorms that come
Once in a generation. As the waking sun
Thrust her fingers between the leaves,
Men arose from the ground, grumbling and stretching.
Smoke arose from cooking fires. The men ate.
The hunters smelled the food, and chewed on the
Leaves they had found on the way, to still the
Sounds of their bellies. They could hear the
Voices of the men, but did not know the meaning
Of their speaking. With shouts, the men walked to the
Slumbering beasts, and climbed upon them.

With roars louder than many great cats, loud as waterfalls or
The great storm winds, the beasts awoke, and the
Hunters fell back in fear. The giant beasts
Spat and belched and lurched.
Smoke poured from their heads in the cool morning air.
Other men took small beasts in their hands, and
With a sound like uncountable angry wasps,
They bit the trees and made them fall.
Some of the giant beasts lifted the trees in their vast claws,
And laid them on the backs of others, which went away,
Down a path wide enough for ten deer.

The hunters withdrew, and fled,
Till the sound of the beasts could not be heard,
And their stunned ears could find again
The click, chirp, and rustle of beetle, bird, and leaf.
They sat on rocks beside a quiet stream and were silent.
Each slaked his thirst and thought on what he had seen.
The oldest spoke first, and with hesitation,
For never in his many years had such a thing been before.
Though he knew not what they should do,
They should do something, for perhaps they had
Displeased the gods. Things had been well for a long time
Until now, and maybe they had become
Complacent, relying on their skills only,
Without proper reverence for the gods.
One man told of a thing he had seen,
How the men-with-tree-eaters had the skin

Of a great cat stretched to dry, and was it not
True, that the great cats had the special favor of the gods,
And may indeed have been gods themselves?
For who could resist the great cats when they wished to eat,
Or who had seen one and lived? Few, and very few.

The father of the motherless boy said nothing,
But remembered the cat, saw again the blood on its fur,
And felt again the fear-stone in his gut.
The power of the cats was indeed great.

Again the men were silent, till one,
A young man and sometimes foolhardy,
Spoke out with vehemence born of his hunger.
If they could kill these men, he said, their
Beasts would not awaken and eat the trees, the trees would
Grow again, and the animals would return.
It would be easy, he said, to kill them
While they slept. With grunts and murmuring
The hunters debated. Such folly!
Or did the young one speak the wisdom of the gods?

The father of the motherless boy kept his
Peace. Had he not seen enough pain and death?
Should he visit on others, mothers and children,
What he had struggled to bear?
He saw again the brokenness of his mother
As she wrapped sons, daughters, and husband
For their burial, then sat, silent and still,
Till she herself lay in her final sleep.
He was not of their clan, and could not sway
Their choice. To speak in favor of the tree-eaters
Would invite suspicion. Still, his heart
Shunned murder.
If they chose killing, he would not.

They chose.

The woman would not leave. Katu knew that he and Batah had tried every trick they could think of to annoy her and driver her away, but without success. The two friends sat by the stream in the late afternoon shadows and discussed their problem while they watched the little fishes dart among the rocks and reeds.

"Remember when we put the snake in the roll of her sleeping mat? When she was away in the forest with the mothers."

"How she ran! And that scream! Everyone came to see."

"And that red face! With the blue eyes shining so round!" The boys were helpless with laughter, but Batah grew serious again. "But it did not work. She did not leave."

"Even when we put the frog into her eating bowl."

"Even the time we turned over her water pot so that her bed and all her things became wet, she did not leave." The boys stared gloomily at the water running by.

"It is not right that she should sing with the women. She is not one of us. And the girls! They are learning things from her. Girls do not need to learn things. Only cooking," said Katu.

Batah sat thinking about the singing, and the soft sounds of the guitar in the cool evenings. "It sounds pretty. Like the birds, or the water in the stream."

"You are soft! Are you a girl now, talking about the sounds of the birds?"

Batah punched his friend's arm. "What are you saying? You like the music too!"

"I don't! I don't like it!"

"Yes you do! And you like it when she smiles at you, to say hello. You do like it! I see your face. You are pretending!" Arguing yielded to wrestling and punching, until both rolled into the stream, splashing and yelling. They scrambled out and lay dripping and breathing hard.

"It is true that the girls do not need a teacher. The boys need a teacher!" said Batah. "They must take this one away and give us a man to teach the boys. Then we can sit in the evenings and sing and laugh the way they do."

Katu lay quiet, looking up at the darkening sky. His friend spoke the truth. It would be good to laugh and sing the way he saw the women and girls doing. Still, he hardened his heart against his friend.

"We do not need the foreign people's singing and laughing. They come to bring change, always change! Do they think their way is better than ours? Why should that be? They tell us about their god, but has not the cat-god been a god good enough for the Bangese people for all the days of our forefathers? Why should he not be good enough for us?" Katu unconsciously echoed the harsh words of some of the fathers, late at night in the men's hut, but deeper still lay his own fear that the woman and her talk of another god might bring on them the wrath of the cat-god, who had left them alone for so many years.

They would simply have to get rid of her. Then everything would go back to normal, to the way it was before.

They lay and watched the stars appearing, and they schemed until they heard the mothers calling them for supper. Calling, always calling. After a suitable delay they went to eat. Further plans could wait.

In truth the woman fascinated them, though neither would ever admit it. In the cool of the evenings they would hear the soft sounds of her guitar and the girls' and women's voices singing. They found her ready smile and cheerful greetings disarming, even though they pretended indifference and merely grunted in return and drove their animals with greater determination as if they didn't have time for speaking to a woman and a foreigner at that. But their hearts yearned for the camaraderie they could see among the women and girls that gathered around the little hut. They deeply envied and resented that their sisters should have the privilege of interaction with her, of learning the things she taught them, of sharing with her the ways of their people. They had watched, as she grew comfortable with their language and customs. They saw their sisters learn crafting skills and proudly show her what they had made, and teaching her as they learned. The boys wanted to teach her their skills and show her the things they could do. But they were caught in a trap, a web of things they had said to one another and in front of witnesses, how she was so ugly and stupid, that she could not possibly have anything to teach a boy of their tribe.

They would simply have to get rid of her. It was the only way to save face.

As Katu ate his supper outside his mother's small cooking hut, he could hear the lady An-nee talking with some of the others. They were discussing the day's yield in the forest. Someone had found a good-sized growth of *yemcho*, an herb that everyone enjoyed, and there was much excitement about a proposed trip to collect as much of it as possible. He heard the woman speak in her strange way.

"Do you think the *yemcho* would grow in my garden? If we bring some of the roots back here?"

"Mmm, one could try," murmured one voice.

"It is always good to try," said another.

"Especially with *yemcho*," said someone else, and they all laughed.

"I am learning where the paths walk through the trees," said Annee, "But I am not certain of the way alone. It is better for me to have the good things growing here."

The women laughed again, but at her words an idea sprang to life in Katu's mind. She must be lost in the forest, he thought, and perhaps the cat-god would take her... but even if he doesn't, she will certainly be lost. She can never come back here, and certainly they will not send someone else to be eaten. Then all will be as before.

As he and Batah lay on their sleeping mats that night, Katu spoke of the wisdom that had come to him.

"I can pretend we have found some *yemcho*, and lead her away into the jungle," Katu suggested.

"No, say rather that one of the women is in trouble and needs her. She is always running to help someone."

"Yes, that is good. I will say my mother has sent me to get her. Then when we are deep into the jungle on a path she will surely not know, I will hide from her. Then she will wander away and be lost."

"When you come home you will know nothing. I also will know nothing, see nothing."

"I won't need to pretend, even: if she is really lost, I won't know where she is. It is perfect."

"There will be a perfect time also."

The boys lay dreaming of the perfect time to come, when all would be as it was before. Perfect.

The time came just a few days later. Most mornings An-nee would go with the other women when they left on their gathering expeditions, but once in a while she would stay behind for one reason or another. This was one of those days. In addition, Katu had not taken out the pigs that morning. The fathers wished to choose one to be slaughtered for the betrothal feast of the chief's younger daughter.

He waited until there was no one in sight, and carefully worked his way around the clearing until he was on the edge of the forest near An-nee's hut. Then he hurried over to the hut, panting as if he had been running. The lady An-nee must come quickly, he said. His mother had sent him to tell her. Hurry, he would lead her to the place.

She scrambled up from the mat where she had been making marks on the white leaves with her marking-stick, and looked at him with her strange blue eyes.

"You must come, lady," he said, his thief of a smile stealing her resolve not to trust him.

"What is wrong, Katu?" she asked, wary of her traitor's heart melting within her. The boy was beautiful, his dark-chocolate skin in superb contrast to his perfect white teeth, but she knew that he and his friend Batah were responsible for many exquisite little tortures she had endured. She had never caught them red-handed, but somehow they were always around when she discovered a snake in her bed or a toad in her plate, and their thinly disguised amusement gave them away every time.

"The mothers need you, lady. I know where the mothers go for the vegetables and herbs. We can find them easily!"

She looked around her, searching for she knew not what answer in the deserted village. What could she do but trust him, though she knew he was not trustworthy? She sighed.

"Okay Katu, you can show me where they are."

His eyes flashed and then he lowered his lashes, demure as a girl, and said, "Come!" and set off into the thickets of brush that loomed so close.

She tried to ask questions as they hurried away down the path, but he would only say, "I will show you," so that she stopped trying and concentrated on keeping up with him. Deeper they went among the trees, farther than she had ever been, and the paths were soon unknown to her, but still they pressed on. The boy began to slow down, and to look about as if in search of something. Finally he stopped. He did not look at her as he said, "Wait, I will find them," but stepped off the path into the thick undergrowth and disappeared from her view.

She waited, thankful at first to be still. She fanned herself with a large leaf and felt the sweat begin to dry on her face even while it trickled down the hollow of her spine. She listened to the silence of the forest that was no silence and began to feel its effect. Tiny rustling, whistling, and chirping sounds of unseen creatures crept into her consciousness, and she gradually grew uneasy.

"Katu?" she called softly. The cathedral hush and green gloom overwhelmed her. Panic gripped her for a moment and she took a hold, told herself to get a grip and retrace their steps. She took a few hesitant steps back along the path, but the thick covering of leathery leaves showed no footprints to help her.

"Katu!" she called again, louder, and heard only stillness and silence, as the invisible inhabitants stopped to hear what new danger might be present here. She would have to help herself. She began to walk slowly back the way they had come.

Two hours later, she knew she was hopelessly lost. The sun above the thick leafy canopy was high overhead and gave no indication of direction. She was desperately thirsty, so the sound of running water drew her. She came to a small stream, and hesitated before drinking, knowing that she risked disease by drinking, and laughed as she found herself wondering which death would be better, death by disease or by thirst... *At least I can still laugh at myself,* she thought.

She bent to cup handfuls of water. As she drank, she caught a sudden movement from the corner of her eye and jumped back – and realized that the dark creature huddled in the shadows on the far bank was her tormentor and erstwhile guide, Katu. His eyes were huge in the gloom and the expression on his face was one of abject misery.

"Katu!" she said. "What are you doing here?"

He crouched even lower, cringing as if he feared she would strike him. She waded into the water and crossed to him. Lifting his chin with one hand, she was startled to see a large tear roll down his brown cheek.

"What is the matter?" she asked.

"We are lost, lady. Katu lost the lady An-nee and then he lost also himself."

Annie climbed onto the protruding tree roots beside the boy and slid her arm around his thin shoulders.

"If we must be lost," she said, "it is good that we are lost together."

The boy began to sob. "It is not good, lady An-nee," he said. "It is wrong. Katu is bad. Katu wished the cat-god to eat the lady An-nee. Now the cat-god will eat Katu also."

She went still with the impact of his words. Sensing the resentment and an undercurrent of ill feeling towards her was something she could put down to paranoia; hearing it spoken aloud was a knife to her heart. With a silent prayer for help, she asked, "Katu, why did you wish that the cat-god would eat me?"

She waited some time for his answer. When it came it was disjointed and hard to follow, but she understood in her youthful wisdom that it was the same reason that people everywhere hate the stranger, the newcomer, the one who upsets the natural slow evolution of their lives and seasons with the changes they bring. They sat quietly together, and he finally rested his head against her arm and looked up at her with eyes that said, *Truce?* In her eyes and her smile he read the reply, *Truce. We are friends.*

They began to try to find their way home. The sun had begun to move towards the west and they tried to head in that direction. Besides, Annie reasoned, the stream they had found had to flow towards the sea and away from the mountains, and they could follow it towards civilization. She could not know that it would take them farther from Kinta village.

They came to a small clearing where they could see that the sun was slanting low between the trees. There was no recognizable feature in the landscape; there had been none for what seemed many hours. Annie sat wearily on a deadfall log. She picked up a large dead leaf and began to fan herself. The boy sank down on his haunches. His face was pale and he looked exhausted. The realization had begun to grow in her that they might be forced to spend the night in the forest, and that she would have to take care of them. The first thing would be to find them something to eat. At least the nights were warm. But what about the possibility that the cat-god *would* get them? She shuddered and forced the thought from her mind. Food.

She got up to start looking.

They ate a meal of herbs and leaves and made themselves a bed and shelter of soft leafy branches in a hollow beneath the deadfall. As the darkness fell with its tropical suddenness they crawled into their space and tried to get comfortable. Both tried to be cheerful and nonchalant, but at some point Annie felt the branches beneath her shaking. She reached out to touch Katu's shoulder and felt the shuddering sobs that racked his small body. Turning over and nestling closer, she wrapped the child in her arms.

"I am so afraid, lady An-nee."

"That's okay, Katu. I am afraid too."

"But I am a man, lady An-nee. The men of my people have courage. They are not afraid."

"You are still a boy, Katu. When you are grown you will see, the fear is there but it does not hold you and make you do what it wants. You can do what is right even when you are afraid. That is the courage of the men. The women, too, have courage, but they are not ashamed to say they also have fear."

The boy was quiet for a long time and Annie thought he might have gone to sleep, until a timid whisper came: "Lady An-nee, can the lady sing the songs of the mothers? The songs they sing at your hut in the evening. The songs give me courage when the night is very dark."

So Annie sang softly, rocking the child gently in their den under the log, and the songs gave them courage when the night grew very dark.

Part VI: Cat

In the first gray of the sun's awakening,
Beneath knives and spears, men fell prey
To the hunters. When once again
The sun's golden touch lay upon the leaves,
It lay also on the ruddy gleam
Of naked bodies splashed with blood.
With bloodied hands,
The hunters ate other men's food, gathered some
For those who awaited them, and took with them
The skin of the great cat.

With careful ritual the tribe offered
Gifts to their gods, purified themselves, and waited.
The animals would surely return.
The forest was cleansed.

High on a far peak stood a tribeless man,
On his back a motherless boy.
He turned away from the gray awakening of the sun,
And chose his path.

Where could she be? How could they even start looking for her? Still he drove like a madman, taking the curves too fast, feeling the tires slipping sideways in the dirt, not caring, feeling an enormous and overwhelming fear of the things he knew happened to people in the jungle. He threw the jeep over the roots and tussocks on the jungle path. When he arrived at the village he slammed to a halt where a knot of men stood together, waiting for him. He leapt from the vehicle and saw by their grave faces that there was still no news. His shoulders sagged and he glanced around, seeing in the distance the women gathered around Katu's mother, who moaned quietly as she rocked back and forth in the dirt. The women made little keening noises as they shared her misery, while the smaller children clustered near their mothers with fear and uncertainty in their great dark eyes.

Ben looked at the men around him, seeing with embarrassment that splatters of dirt from his mad entrance coated their skins. Remembering his manners, he greeted them respectfully and apologized for his haste. They nodded graciously, accepting and compassionate; they understood that he was betrothed to the young woman. He was surprised but said nothing, thinking that they must have assumed so from the many times he had visited Annie. He told them he had heard the news from a search party he had met on the mountain trail, and they told him what was being done to help find the woman and the child. Nothing more could be done until the most recent group of searchers returned; another group would leave immediately, but for now they were resting and eating to give them strength for another journey. Would the brother Ben like to take some refreshment also?

They ate and drank, and spoke of other times and searches, yet their talk and their patience maddened Ben; he felt he must do something besides wait; at least he could drive the logging roads in case she found a road and began to walk that way. Bowing and thanking the men, he explained his plan and took his leave.

Miles and miles of red dirt tracks, rutted and potholed, craters and canyons frozen in time since the last rains, dust and heat, flies, biting gnats, sweat burning in tired eyes, endless tracts of green and growing things, the fecundity of the forest an obscenity, a living wall keeping secret living mysteries, hidden deaths, *please God, not deaths, not Annie, not the boy, but specially not Annie, please God, I'm sorry I didn't listen to her, she's right, I need You, I need her but really she's right, I need You. I am so sorry, so sorry. I am so dumb. Why didn't I come to see her before? Stubborn pride! What was I thinking? If you help us find her that will be enough for me, just to know she's okay, I won't try to be with her again, I mean, I don't blame her for not wanting to marry me, just save her, rescue her, please God. God, it's getting dark, how can they stay in the forest through the night, they won't make it, please take care of them God.*

Over and over the litany of fear and contrition, over and over through the long night, when finally he slept curled beneath his old coat in the back of the jeep, weary beyond weariness.

Pale light filtered through the trees when he awoke, startled, and sat up, bleary-eyed and blinking up at the bird whose screeching had disturbed him. It bobbed its head and looked at him, muttering to itself about the odd thing sitting on the trail, before flying off with a final scream. Ben sat in the quiet, feeling the cool fingers of a light breeze touch the dew on his clothes, thankful that it meant fewer mosquitoes, wondering where to go, what to do, how to deal with the black hole of failure and loss that swallowed rational thought and every other feeling.

Perhaps they had found them by now. He started up the jeep and realized he had very little fuel left; he would have to give up the search and trust the villagers and their knowledge of the forest. Slowly he returned to Kinta; there was no news. Defeated, his heart torn beyond bearing, he made his farewells. He explained to the people that he had come yesterday to say goodbye to them all, not knowing then that the woman and the boy had been lost. He was returning to the land of his father, to care for his father's parents, and to learn the ways of his father's people at the schools there. He would return after many moons had passed. They greeted him with dignity, subdued in their mourning and the guilt that accrued to them from Batah's complicity in the plot against the woman. When the boy had told them with tears of fear and anxiety about his part in Katu's plan, each man knew in his heart that his words against her had found their home in the boys' minds. It was a communal sin, and a shared sorrow, deepened by the pain they read in the brother Ben's eyes; a city man, true, and not of their village, but still a man of their own people, whose desired woman may have been lost for the sake of their pride.

If he had married her, whether they lived at Kinta or not, things would have been different: she would not have been the single woman with no family who had caused them so much consternation. Those who thought thus sighed and said nothing, for the sake of saving the brother Ben's face, for they knew how long it could take to save a high bride price, and none could imagine what sort of bride price a woman like that could command. They had begun to debate this issue with the man who wanted her for his third wife. Though he disguised it well, his relief when he had heard of her betrothal was great. For the sake of face he could not with honor withdraw his offer, but he had begun to realize that his pride was greater than his purse.

Ben left them then, not knowing, carrying with him the mourner's burden of pain and what-if guilt. On the following day he flew to his father's country, to learn the ways of his father's people at the university where his father had studied, and to learn for himself the depths of culture fatigue and aloneness.

There is little to be said about Annie and Katu's second day in the jungle. Heat and sweat, flying biting things, eating green things and stumbling between green things and smelling the green, growing things until Annie began to dream of deserts and mountains and snow, of Kansas plains and ocean breezes. Even the prayers in her heart and mind became blurred and unfocused, a litany of *Oh God, please help us.*

The boy Katu tried to be a man, tried so hard to be a man, but by late afternoon his limbs shook with exhaustion and he could barely chew on the leaves and herbs the girl brought him. They sat on the moss-covered roots of a giant tree, and she held him, and told him stories.

"Lady An-nee, can your God save us from the jungle and from the cat-god?"

"Yes, Katu, he is greater than the cat-god, and he can save us."

"Why has he not saved us yet, lady?"

"Perhaps it is because we have not asked him out loud. I have been praying in my heart, but perhaps it would be better for us – you and me – to ask out loud."

"That is a true thing. I will ask him too. But will he know who I am if I speak to him?"

"Yes, he knows who you are. Remember I said to you he is greater than the cat-god? He knows all things and all people. He knows where the village is and he knows where we are now. We can ask him to help us and to show us how to get home."

The child looked up at her face and she saw such hope and trust in his eyes that her heart feared. *Oh God, I know you can save us – change my doubting heart! Rescue us, please!*

Katu closed his eyes and folded his hands together as he had seen her do. "Mighty God of the lady An-nee, this is Katu, a man of the Clearing people. I did not speak to you before, but she says it is good for me to speak to you and that you will know who I am. I am sorry that I tried to make the lady An-nee be lost and eaten. I know that she is yours. She says you are greater than the cat-god and so I am asking you to defeat him for us and to bring us back to the village of our people."

He opened one eye and glanced at her. "Is that enough?"

"Yes, Katu, it is enough. He hears." They sat quietly together, leaning against the tree, and she sang softly the songs of her faith until he fell asleep against her shoulder.

She noticed first the quiet - the hush of no bird song, no bug chirp, no monkey screech - and the hair on her arms and neck began to prickle.

He stood still as the trees of the breathing
Forest, the spear in his hand a liana in the shadows.
A smell was there, like no other. A stink of fear.
A small sound – a child's whimper – and a sudden movement
Between far trees. A color not of the jungle –
He moved as a liquid shadow, swift as a bird, and saw
A woman, a child, the cat –
Crouched to spring, its tail flicking, the fearsome teeth –

"What is it, lady?" The boy sat up in alarm, immediately sensing her unease. Were the shadows playing tricks on her eyes, or was there a movement among the trees across the little clearing? *Dear God, could it be possible - ?* She heard the hiss of the child's indrawn breath and knew he saw it too, the velvet gleam of fur, golden eyes, the huge paws kneading the leaves as the muscles bunched to spring – they both leapt to their feet and the cat backed off momentarily, then crouched lower as its tail twitched. She tried to turn, to shield the boy with her body, knowing it was futile, saw the flash of something fly across the clearing, and there was a spear, and the cat was dying, a last agonized roar, and a cough, and blood, and a man, small and dark and almost naked, with a great knife in his hand.

The spear flashed, and drove into the deep chest
In the silken hollow of shoulder and breast. The beast
Shuddered, fell back,
Roared its agony, then coughed and was still,
As the bright fresh blood stained the leaf floor
And the golden eyes glazed and died.
He turned, his knife still in his hand.
The woman saw the knife, knew it had sprung there as
The spear was released, saw the hunter crouching,
Still and ready, and felt the trembling of her limbs. The child
Who clung to her shook with dry and silent gasps of fear, and
Stared at the bleeding thing across the clearing.
The woman was like none the man had seen,
Tall and slim as a sapling in the forest, and her hair white
As the underbelly of a deer, though she seemed young.
Her arms and face were the pale brown of one who was ill,
Though the child was dark of skin and hair.
The eyes, too, were strange, the color of the
Daylight above the tallest trees.
She wore clothes of thin flower-colored skins.
She tried to speak, but only strange sounds came,
While a rainfall of tears
Fell from the eyes of daylight.
He turned to the cat. It lay dead,
Warm blood cooling, congealing.
The hunter laid his hand on the great head.

In his heart, fierce pride fought sorrow,

That he could kill this god of the forest.
With a stroke of the knife he opened the belly
And gutted the animal in a hot rush of
Fluids and stink, then shouldered the carcass.
He gestured to the woman and child to
Follow.

They followed.

He led them to the place where his son lay hidden, and after they had shared meat he worked with the skin of the great cat, cleaning it and pegging it out to dry. He saw and approved, that the woman collected leaves and grass to make a bed for the children. She talked softly with the older boy as she helped them prepare for rest.

"You can rest here tonight, Katu; we will be safe. Then tomorrow we will try again to get home."

The boy was quiet and sober. He looked up at her with his beautiful eyes, and in them she saw a different light. "Lady An-nee, it is true. Your God is greater than the cat-god. Did he not bring the hunter to kill the cat at just the right moment?"

"Yes, Katu, He did. I was fearful, yet He rescued us as we prayed. I am very thankful to Him."

"Lady, I was fearful too. But we did not run away. We had courage." She saw that the knowledge that he had passed the test filled him with deep satisfaction and peace.

"Yes Katu, we had courage. Trust in Jesus gives you courage too."

"I trust Him, lady. I will ask Him again to help us to find our village, and He will do it!" So they prayed, and were thankful. The boy settled into the bed they had made with a deep sigh of relief. The hunter's small boy stared at him with his big eyes, and Katu grinned at him and patted the bed next to him. The little one decided it was good, and they snuggled down together. They soon slept.

The woman crouched near the children's bed and watched the man with her strange daylight eyes, wary as a deer, until the eyes grew heavy with sleep, and she lay down with the children and slept as the velvet night closed over them.

The hunter watched, and
Pondered the puzzle of the woman. Even the boy
Was not as his own people, the child's face
Sharp as the hawk's, and not softly rounded.
Were they of the sky?
Yet the woman knew some of the ways of the forest -
The making of beds for children,
The herbs to gather for food.
The morning would give an answer.
He slept, crouching still near the small fire,
Ears alert for any sound.

In the early light he looked, and found
The place where they had come, the crushed
Leaf, the bruised moss, the marks of her foot-clothes in the soft soil.
He tended the small fire, roasting meat from his kill,
And pondered again how to return these sky people –
Hawk boy, eyes-of-daylight woman -
To their own place.

The thought came to him then,
That perhaps in their eating of the trees
The great beasts and their men
Had opened the place in the forest so wide
That these sky people had fallen down. If
He should return them there
Perhaps there would be a way for them
To get back to their place in the sky?
He could find no other ideas, though
This one filled him with unease -
The open place of the sky was a place
Of evil and sorrow. Yet if such were their place,
Then better they should return there.
Perhaps he should not have saved them,
But their lives were now in his hand, since he had
Taken their lives from the cat god. Perhaps he would be
Punished for making such a choice, but how
Could he say what was in his heart?
Though it had not been the way of his people,
To care for strangers and not to murder them,
This had grown within him,

The fruit of his pain.

When they awoke,
They could tell him nothing, though
The woman with gestures and strange noises
Tried to speak. The hawk boy looked hopeful also;
Clearly they thought he might know
Something. Had he not shown them his
Prowess? He was Ahnaket, the hunter.
He gave them food, snuffed the fire,
Shouldered the skin of the great cat,
Led the way to the place of the open sky.

Refreshed as she was by the rest and the food, Annie struggled to keep following as the hunter strode rapidly along winding paths she could barely see. She was taller than he, so that branches and vines struck her face and shoulders in places where he easily walked beneath them. He seemed immensely strong, walking lightly and easily even bearing the burden of the cat's still-wet skin in addition to his bag and spear. She meanwhile carried the hunter's small child on her back, and tried also to help and support Katu, but their strength began to give out early on this their third day, so that the hunter had to pause more and more frequently to wait for them. Finally when the sun was high overhead he stopped alongside a stream, and once again produced a meal for them from the pouch slung about his shoulders. They were so tired that they could barely eat, though the hunter urged them with gestures to eat and drink, and then indicated that they should lie down and rest also. They did so with relief. After what Annie guessed was about an hour they set off again. This time the small man carried his child also. She felt ashamed to be so weak, even as she was awed by his strength and grateful for his awareness of their exhaustion. She had no idea where he was taking them, nor why a man would be alone with a child in the jungle, but he seemed to know where he was going and how to take care of them all, and that was enough for her.

Sometime in the middle of the afternoon, the man stopped and gave the child to Annie again. He seemed more wary, and walked more slowly and cautiously forward, until Annie realized that ahead of them she could see a great clearing where the sun shone brightly. The man began to gesture towards the clearing and up towards the sky, and to speak to her as if to explain something to her, but to her ears he remained incomprehensible. She was suddenly startled to hear the sounds of human voices in the distance, and she glanced down at Katu to see that he too heard, and his face lit up.

"It is our people, lady An-nee, we are home!" he said, and his weariness was forgotten as he ran forward towards the sunlight and the voices of his people.

"Mother! Mother!" he called, all thoughts of manhood forgotten, just a child, lost and now found. He ran on ahead, and soon Annie heard him talking excitedly and men's voices in reply, as she followed him towards the light. Suddenly they were in the clearing, and the men with Katu were in uniform, and armed with rifles, and an angry shout arose from them as they saw the hunter behind her, and they raised the rifles and aimed them at him, and even as she saw him drop the cat's skin and lift his spear, she heard the roar of the rifles, and she heard herself shouting NO!! as she dropped the child she carried and ran to stop them, and felt something slam into her, and fell into blackness.

Part VII: Scars

Ahnaket, the hunter, swam to thought
On a river of fiery pain whose flames
Ate at limbs and body. He grunted, struggled to
Move, could not. His head, his body,
All were restrained. He moved his eyes, and saw
No tree, no leaf, only a pale and smooth place
Without one familiar feature.
A strange squeak and rustle approached,
 Like no animal he had ever heard;
A sweat of fear sheened his skin
As he strained again to free himself
And felt only his weakness.
A face appeared within his view.
The face was a hawk face, a face like that
Of the boy from the sky.
Was this the place of punishment
To which the gods had sent him?
A cold hard stick was pushed into the hunter's mouth –
He spat it out violently,
Glared fiercely at the stranger,
Cursed him in guttural tones.
God or no god, he would not surrender
Easily to their torture. The face held
Disgust. The person left,
Babbling loudly with a woman's voice.
The hunter felt the fear of prey-being.
He struggled weakly to free himself –
Could not.
He lay in the sweat of his fear.

As consciousness slowly returned Annie felt first the pain, and then smelled the sharp pungency of a hospital; as memory awoke she heard again the roar of the rifles, her own shout, and the shrill cries of the boy Katu and the hunter's child, and the horror of what had happened made her groan with anguish. She was, apparently, still alive: what about the others? She could see nothing. There was terrible pain in her head and in her right arm when she tried to lift it; it seemed that it was strapped down, so perhaps her shoulder or collarbone was broken. Her left arm could move, though she could feel the slight weight and drag of an intravenous drip line. With her left hand she explored her face and found her head and eyes were covered with bandages. Her mouth felt so dry! Her seeking fingers crept outward in hopes of finding water. Instead they encountered the soft warmth of another hand, and a cheery voice greeted her in English.

"How happy we are that you are awake at last! Two days you have been sleeping," a woman's voice cried. "You must want a drink very badly, poor dear." Annie heard the soft metallic chink of a spoon on a glass, and the cool freshness of water trickled slowly into her eagerly gulping mouth. "Today when the doctor comes he will take off the bandages and we will see your pretty face again."

"Katu – the boy – is he safe? The baby – the hunter - where are they? Are they okay?" Her words were barely a whisper and Annie could not recognize her own voice, but the woman understood.

"The children are here too, my dear. They are very well. You are at the best hospital in Bangita," she said proudly. She began checking her patient's vital signs, and Annie could hear the scratching noise of her pen on the chart as she wrote.

"The hunter - did he die? Did they shoot him?"

"That man? They shot him, yes, but he did not die. He is here too, and they have him under guard. They want him to live so that he can go on trial," the nurse replied, and Annie heard sudden venom in her voice. She was puzzled.

"What did he do?"

"Hmph! What did he do? He killed all those men at the logging camp, that's what he did! He and his jungle friends. Plus they caught him with that poached skin, still fresh – they will get him for that, even if they can't prove he was there when the men were killed. My cousin's husband was up there and they killed him too. Just a truck driver, he was, just doing his job, and speared like an animal. I wish they would catch all of them. Wild as animals themselves, those jungle people are. Hanging is too good for them! Okay my dear, we will soon have you up and on your feet. The doctor makes his round in about half an hour and I will see you then."

Annie heard the squeak of the woman's shoes disappearing down the hallway, and lay in the darkness of her bandaged eyes, and the pain in her heart seemed less bearable than the pain of her injuries.

When the doctor came, he and the nurse carefully unwound the bandages from Annie's head; she was thankful that she was able to open her eyes a little and see things around her, though the light seemed unbearably bright.

"You have a bullet wound on the side of your head. We feared that it may affect your eyesight – but you can see me, can you not? That is excellent news." The doctor was cool and professional, but Annie saw the flash of sympathy on the nurse's face when she looked at the wound, and she thought that *pretty* was not a word she would use again.

"We were able to stitch and repair most of the damage, but I am afraid a small part of the top of your ear has been lost. When your hair grows again, you will not see it. Please do not be alarmed when you see yourself – your face is very swollen and discolored with bruising. Just remember that you are very lucky to be alive." He turned his attention to her shoulder, peeling back the dressing, and appeared to be satisfied with what he saw.

"Your collarbone was broken by another bullet. We were able to get the bullet out and put you back together with pins and screws. You will need to have some physical therapy to get things working right again." He stopped then and looked at her, and she saw beneath the professionalism his deep compassion. "Your healing will take time and love and patience, Miss Ah-nee. Do you have family here in BC who will help you? You must realize that in fact we have had no way to identify you – just the child Katu who told us your name."

The reality of what he was saying was barely comprehensible to

Annie, but she assured him that she knew people in BC and felt sure they would be able to help her, if someone could help her make some phone calls, perhaps? Oh, and her name was Annie Robbins, she was a US citizen, and she had medical insurance to help her pay for her treatment.

"We can talk about payment later, but as soon as you are feeling well enough the police would like to talk to you about what happened. Do you feel like you could answer some questions? A detective has been waiting for some time for you to wake up."

"Yes, that will be fine." Annie agreed weakly. Her mind whirled with broken images and memories, and the struggle to grasp the meaning of the doctor's words. The doctor and nurse left the room. Shortly afterwards the nurse returned with another man. Though he wore a plain civilian suit, his military bearing was obvious.

"Good morning, Miss Robbins. I am Inspector Vidu. I need to ask you a few questions if you are feeling well enough." The detective's words were polite, but his eyes were dark gimlets and his jaw a steel trap. Annie thought she had better feel well enough, regardless of the pain in her head and the trepidation in her heart.

"Tell me how you came to be in that place at that time, please. Leave out nothing. I will be recording our conversation." He set up a small tape recorder on the table beside the bed. Step by step he took her through the story of Katu's plan of losing her in the jungle, until they came to the time when she and Katu met the hunter and his child.

"So, you think you had been lost for two days?"

"Yes, sir, we had spent one night in the jungle on our own."

"And the hunter found you – did he have the cat skin and the child with him at the time?"

"Oh no, it wasn't like that. We were in this little clearing; we were so tired by then and we had stopped for a rest." She closed her eyes and the memory came back clear and vivid, so that the skin on her forearms prickled again as she remembered realizing that they were not alone, seeing the cat across the clearing. "It got so quiet, creepy quiet, and I realized something was wrong, and I looked and there was the cat getting ready to pounce on us. He must have been able to smell how tired and scared we were... even when we spoke and got up he was still ready to spring on us... and then the spear came out of nowhere and the hunter was there, and the cat was dying…" She shuddered deeply, with the fear and the knowledge that they had narrowly escaped death.

"He saved our lives," she added simply, looking up at the hard face and dark eyes. There was no reaction, but he simply said, "Continue. What happened next?"

"He skinned the cat, and then he took us to where his little boy was. The baby was hiding, so still you would never know he was there. The man made a fire and he fed us all, and we went to sleep there. That was when he cleaned the cat's skin. When we woke up, he fed us again and took us to the big clearing where the police were."

"How long did this take?"

"We walked nearly all day – I suppose about seven hours?"

"Why did he take you to that place? Had you ever been there before?"

"I had never been there. I don't know why he took us there – we didn't speak each other's language so we really couldn't communicate. I don't know where he thought we were from" She closed her eyes again, and frowned as she tried to recall exactly what he had said and done. She remembered his gestures, how he had kept pointing up to the sky and then to her and Katu, but she had no idea what he had meant. She explained this to the cold man sitting beside her. She found herself wanting to defend him, the small, strong man who had held their lives in his hand and cared for them, strangers, as tenderly as he cared for the small child he carried with him.

"When you came to the clearing, what did you see?"

"At first we didn't see anything, but we heard voices, and Katu ran ahead because he thought we were home, back at the village, and then when the hunter and I got to the edge of the trees I saw that the people there were in uniform. As soon as they saw the hunter and his spear they wanted to shoot him – why did they do that? He started trying to defend himself. He was lifting his spear, and I tried to stop them from shooting… I guess that wasn't very smart, since I got shot as well…" Her voice trailed off; she felt so tired, and her swollen face ached from the effort of talking… She awoke, startled, and saw that the man had left and taken his recording equipment with him. She lay and thought about the strange events of the past few days, about the strange man from the jungle.

He had seemed so certain about where to go. If he knew about the place, did he know about the people that had been killed there, by people like him, armed with spears and knives? Perhaps he had been one of them, but surely then he must have known that it was a dangerous place for him to be? Yet he knew that his world and theirs met there, in that clearing of blood and sorrow, and he faced the danger for their sake. Why would one do that for a stranger?

A meal was brought to her. She ate awkwardly with her left hand, but the food, simple as it was, tasted good to her – her first real meal in many days. As she finished her meal, a woman came into her room. She introduced herself as Soolan; she was the hospital chaplain. They talked for a while; Soolan seemed to know something of her situation, and offered to help her locate her friends or relatives in Bangita. She had brought a telephone directory with her, and a cordless phone, and they started with the Palmers' home number.

"It's just ringing," she said, and then she listened more intently and canceled the call. "The number has been disconnected," she said.

"We could try the mission office," suggested Annie. A tiny tickle of concern began to grow, as she remembered that she hadn't seen the Palmers since before Christmas. "By the way," she asked, "What is the date today?"

"It is June the fifteenth," Soolan said casually as she keyed in the numbers for the mission office, and didn't notice Annie's little gasp of shock as she realized how much time she had lost. How little meaning the passage of time had in Kinta, in the way she had always understood it. The steady turn of the earth, the sun, the moon, and the stars had given them the rhythms of their days, and six months had gone by with little to mark their passing.

"This one, too, is disconnected," the chaplain told her, and Annie could see the concern in her eyes. "Who else can we try?"

Annie thought of Ben – but could she call him when he clearly did not want to contact her? She could of course call the American embassy, and probably would need to soon, since her passport was in Kinta village with no way for her to retrieve it. What about one of the churches she had attended with the Palmers? She had been at Pastor Bob's church just twice, and with the size of his congregation she felt sure he would not remember her. Ms. Charlotte would remember her, but Annie knew she disapproved of her. That would not be a pleasant experience.

What about Alicia Williams? She seemed so efficient, knew the Bangese ways; she had told Annie to call. It was almost a year since their journey together – how would she feel about Annie calling her now? Somehow the fact that she was from her hometown helped Annie make the decision. They found her name in the phone book and dialed the number. Alicia answered, remembered Annie, and said she would be there as soon as she could.

"Is there anything else I can get for you in the meantime?" asked Soolan, her dark eyes warm with sympathy. "I have several religious writings here with me, in case you would like to read?" She rummaged in her capacious shoulder bag and pulled out slim paperbound volumes. Annie saw that they were a series called *Readings from the Holy Books*. Among the volumes Soolan held were the Tripitaka, the Book of Mormon, the Qur'an, the Bhagavad Gita, and the Bible, and she fanned them out for Annie's choice. Annie gratefully took the little *Selections from the Bible*, surprised at her emotional response to seeing a Bible again.

"Thank you so much, Soolan," she said. "You have been such a comfort to me."

"It is little that I can do to bring comfort; I am glad to be of some assistance to you. I will come again when I can."

"Do you think you can visit the hunter who was shot? Is he allowed to have visitors?"

"I will ask to be allowed. I do not speak his language but perhaps I can do something to help him," Soolan promised, and took her leave.

Nurses came then to help Annie get out of bed and take a bath. Supporting her and the paraphernalia of drips, taking off the sling that immobilized her arm, they cheerfully bustled her through the awkwardness and embarrassment and the horror of the smashed and distorted face she glimpsed in the mirror, tufts of bloodied hair on one side, shaved bald on the other. Their gentle touch and the soothing warm water, the smell of soap, the feeling of clean hair, refreshed her and at the same time brought her to a level of tearful gratitude that seemed to her pathetic. She lay back in the bed afterwards, exhausted, wondering how things could have come to this, how it could all be resolved; wondering most of all what had happened to the Palmers and the support system she had talked about so eagerly.

"Girl, you sure know how to get yourself in a mess. Just look at that face! You look like you been up against old Sugar Ray for a few rounds. And don't you know you gotta shave BOTH sides of your head to get the Mohawk look?" Clicking her tongue in dismay, Alicia Williams took hold of Annie's hand and shook her head at the sorry sight before her. Annie laughed weakly, but the laughter became tears, and she grasped Alicia's hand and shook with sobs. The other woman pulled a chair up close to the bed and held her. "That's it, honey; you just cry it all out. You've had a horrible time, and there's no use in pretending otherwise."

"Miss Alicia, thank you so much for coming. I didn't know who to call..."

"Well first up you gonna quit that Miss Alicia stuff – my friends call me Lisha. Now, what happened to get you into this mess? Start at the top – I got all the time in the world. I don't hear from you in a year and next thing you're all shot up in the hospital. Good grief, girl, this has got to be a good story."

Sometime during the telling of the long story, hospital staff brought dinner for Annie. As soon as Lisha saw what was on the plate, she announced that no self-respecting woman could possibly get healthy eating that stuff, and she would be back in a little bit with some real food. True to her word, within the hour she was back. From a large bag she took a fork and a covered dish containing homemade barbecued pork, potato salad, and collard greens.

"Collard greens? Where did you get those?" Annie took the dish, inhaling the delicious fragrance of the food.

"Tom and I grow this stuff at home. We figured if we wanted to be at home here we should just bring some of home here with us. I like Bangese food a lot, but there's some things we just miss too much. Come on, girl, eat!"

Annie ate. When she had finished, Lisha took the dish and the fork and, wrapping them in a plastic bag, she dropped them back in her bag.

"Well, baby, it's late and I'm gonna need some beauty sleep, so close up those sorry blue eyes of yours and I will see you in the morning." She bent down and gently hugged the younger woman. "You'll be okay, Annie. We Georgia women are tough." And with a smile and a wave, she headed out the door. The warmth of her personality vibrated in the room long after she had gone. Annie closed her sorry blue eyes, and slept.

In the morning, Lisha was back. She brought with her a nightgown, robe, and slippers. She dug into the big squashy bag she carried and took out a comb and a pair of scissors.

"I may not be the best hairdresser in the world, but anybody could do a better job than I'm looking at right now," she said, and she carefully and neatly trimmed and styled Annie's hair to balance and cover the shaven right temple.

"This is the one and only time I will ever think a comb-over is a good idea."

She pulled out a makeup bag and gently applied eye makeup, lip gloss, blush. She had even brought a hand mirror, and she silently handed it to Annie, who looked for a long time, first at one side of her face, then at the other, mottled in shades of blue and green beneath the makeup. Her eye was bloodshot and almost closed; the stitches along the bloody tip of her torn ear looked ragged. She looked up at Lisha's brown eyes, saw the eyebrows raised expectantly. "Well?"

"Lisha, it's so much better than it was – thank you so much. I just didn't think my looks mattered to me, and now that I look so ugly, I am shocked at how bad it makes me feel. I don't want anyone to see me like this."

"Annie, here's what I want you to remember: when people treat you different because you don't look a certain way, you don't have a problem, they do. I had to learn this a long time ago and I'm passing the lesson along to you, free and for nothing. Your face will heal and you will look almost the same as you did before, but there are people who will always look different, and just think about them and take care you don't treat them different. And you will never be ugly, because what's inside a person shows through no matter what happens on the outside."

They looked at each other, and a slow smile grew across each face. Lisha pulled the chair up to the side of the bed.

"Right, lecture over. Now, when I got home last night I checked the Internet for your Mr. Palmer. Honey, I have bad news, I'm afraid. Turns out Mr. Palmer was killed in a car wreck in the US in January. His wife never came back here, and they closed up the mission office here. There was a bit in the BC paper about it. How come nobody came out to get you?"

"Poor Mr. Palmer! I have been wondering what happened, but I never thought…" Annie's eyes filled with tears. So much made sense now! Yet Lisha was right, surely someone should have known about her out in Kinta? She thought back to conversations she had had with Tom Palmer, when they were debating her removal to Kinta, and finally understood what he had been doing.

"I guess he brought me to Bangita and took me out to Kinta without the church leaders even knowing about it. He was going to try to persuade them after it was already a done deal. What's that thing people say? It's easier to ask forgiveness than permission? I never knew how horribly that could backfire. So that means I'm on my own. Oh man! What a mess!" Suddenly she began to laugh, and soon Lisha was laughing too, and they laughed until their faces were wet with tears and their sides ached and Annie's head and shoulder throbbed.

"Lisha, can you do something else for me?" she asked when they were quiet again. "I need to know what has happened to Katu and the hunter's little baby. The nurse said they were here in the hospital. I'm pretty sure they weren't injured though, so what will they do with them? They surely can't keep them here indefinitely."

"Okay, I will go visit them right now. See what I can find out." Without hesitation she strode off down the hallway to find the pediatric wards. She was back within the half hour.

"Right. I got to see them both and they are fine, as you said, not injured, nothing a bit of nourishing food won't fix. Katu was just sitting moping in the corner, looking sadder than a wet weekend. I asked the nurse to tell him that you had sent me and you should have seen him smile - he thought you were dead for sure. The nurse said he was saying over and over, 'She's not dead! She's not dead!' What's that about?"

Annie told her about Katu and Batah's plot to have her eaten by the cat. "But I guess he changed his mind about wanting me to die. We had a really good time together in the jungle – apart from, you know, being lost… It would have been rather ironic if I had been killed by the police instead."

Lisha shook her head. "Like I said before, you sure know to get in a mess. Okay, here's the bad part. I asked them how long the kids would be staying here. She says, if their parents don't come to claim them within the week they will send them out to the foster home system."

"No! We can't let that happen! What can we do? We've got to get them out of here!"

"Don't panic, girl! We'll get them out somehow. We obviously can't get Katu's mama here by Friday, and the baby's daddy is somewhere here in the hospital, and he obviously can't take the baby."

'But it's not that far to Kinta – only about five hours. Couldn't we get a four-wheel drive from somewhere, then go and get Takatu and get her back here in time?"

"Don't talk like a crazy woman. I don't know how to get there and you are not going anywhere in that condition. I've got an idea that I think will work. I'll ask Julak to help me. She helps me out at the house. We'll come up with something. And what about you? When can we get you out of here?"

"I'll ask the doctor tomorrow. Lisha, you are awesome. I've never had a friend like you before."

"Honey, that's because we lived in Atlanta before." Annie's eyes widened, and then she saw the twinkle in her friend's eye, and once again they laughed till the tears ran down their cheeks.

Other strangers had come and gone,
Touched him, probed the many
Wounds he felt with fiery pain.
Some stung him like bees and
He would sleep, and wake
Thick of mind and tongue.
Some placed cold stones in his mouth that
His fever melted to water. They
Loosened his bonds; he moved his head,
Yet still he saw in this place
Nothing familiar. Memories like dreams
Moved through his waking thoughts

In confusion and despair.
The child – his child, his own child -
Was surely lost, and the
Woman with eyes of daylight, the
Hawk-faced boy. He had chosen
With all the knowledge and
Wisdom he possessed;
The choices had been wrong. He wished for
Death; yet what if this was indeed death?
Was he condemned to eternal torture?
In the dark of the night, the walls,
Smooth and hard, cold as stone,
Echoed with his howl of pain and despair.

Annie heard the howl, the sound of a soul in torment. The night was dark. She listened, and again it came, and she knew who it was who howled in such primeval agony. Carefully she sat up, and swung her feet over the edge of the bed. Thankful that she no longer had to fight with the drip, she awkwardly draped Lisha's robe around her shoulders and shuffled her feet into the slippers. Her head swam and throbbed. Slowly then, like an old, old person, she thought, she made her way down the dimly lit halls, following the sound of the hunter's cry. She drew near a corner, and heard the angry voice of a night nurse, warning the man to be quiet or they would come with an injection needle and knock him out again. She knew he could not understand the words, but the threat in the voice was clear, and he grew quiet. She heard the nurse's footsteps dying away down the hall, and slowly she resumed her shuffle towards the room where he lay.

The shouts quieted his howls,
Yet still his heart cried out in the
Torment of his soul, How long?
Could he never feel again the soft
Earth beneath his feet, the brush of
Wind on his cheek? Suddenly
He knew someone to be close by.

In the dim light he saw
The pale woman with eyes of daylight.
He saw that her face was twisted,
Swollen as one with a wound.
She lived! She whispered with her
Strange words, and laid
Cool fingers on his cheek. He read
Compassion in her eyes, and knew
Hope again. She held a cup to his mouth,
Trickled in a little water. She held some
Soft wet thing to his cheeks, forehead, hands,
So that he felt a little cool wind touch his skin.
He saw that she was weak and slow from her wounds.
She laid her hand over his, whispered her
Strange words, looked a thousand words with her
Strange eyes. Left. Strangely comforted,
Ahnaket slept.

The next morning the doctor told Annie that she could go home in a day or two.

"We need to be satisfied that your wounds are healing with no infection. The metal plate in your shoulder will have to remain there, and the stitches will dissolve on their own, so you must rest and eat properly and start on your therapy in a little while. Soon you will be your old self again. I see your friend has done your hair – it looks very nice," he said, and he smiled encouragingly, knowing that the mind too must heal, and not only the body.

"Thank you, Doctor, you are very kind. May I ask you something? Are you the doctor that is taking care of the hunter? Can you tell me how he is doing? And what about his little boy?" asked Annie.

"I was not appointed to his case, but as far as I know he is making progress. He is out of his natural element, of course, and doesn't understand what we are doing to him. He is very distressed."

"Do you think I would be allowed to go and see him? Maybe I could take his little boy to see him – that would make him feel better, don't you think? And maybe I could take care of the little boy when I get out of here – please can you arrange that for me?"

"But I heard this morning that both of the boys were claimed by their mothers. We were very pleased. It is very sad when we have a child who is not claimed by his or her parents."

Annie wasn't sure if she should be glad or horrified by the news – did Takatu really hear about Katu being in the hospital and come to get him? And how could the hunter's child's mother have come? If not, who could have taken the children? She buried her distress and prayed for their safety.

Later that morning the nurse brought her a cordless telephone, saying she had a call.

"Hey Annie, this is Lisha. I won't be able to come by the hospital today – something has come up and I can't get away. Did the doctor say when you could get out?"

"Hey Lisha! Yeah, he says tomorrow or the next day."

"Okay baby, now you just rest and I will come see you or pick you up in the morning, and you are coming home with me, okay?"

"Oh, Lisha, thanks so much - thanks for everything."

The rest of the morning dragged. Annie read a few old magazines, watched some boring TV, and missed Lisha's friendly banter. Her wounds itched and she had to resist the urge to scratch at them. She had time to think about all the people she had lost and now missed with fierce longing. Even cool, distant Mr. Palmer - how awful that he had died and she hadn't even known it! She saw from her reflection in the mirror that the swelling in her face was going down, but still her cheek was puckered, and her hair and ear would never be the same. Oh, well, what did it matter? There was nobody to care what she looked like. Self-pity moved in and reigned supreme.

The aide that collected her lunch tray told her that Dr. Zagad said she had permission to visit the jungle man in room 16, down the hall. Annie was startled and suddenly energized by the news. She put on her robe as best she could and shuffled down the hall, holding the wall for support. Her weakness still surprised her.

She knocked gently on the door and entered the room. The man's eyes sparked with recognition when he saw her. She saw that the bandage holding his head immobile had been removed, and that he could now turn his head, though his body and limbs were still strapped firmly to the bed, and she knew that, besides the fact that they feared he would escape, they feared that he would tear the stitches in his extensive wounds. The shades were drawn across the window, and she went over and drew them back and rolled up the blind beneath. Outside, the sun shone through the leaves of a tree whose branches brushed against the window pane. She heard a sound and turned back to the man lying in the bed, and saw that his chest heaved with restrained sobs and tears trickled down his face. He looked up at her with gratitude and wonder, so that she too was moved to tears. She sat by the bed and laid her hand over his where it lay on the bed, as he gazed and gazed at sunlight playing on leaves.

In a little while she took up the water glass and offered it to him.

"Water?" she said. He frowned at the word, but recognized the cup and opened his mouth to let her trickle some water between his lips. "Water," she said again, and sprinkled a few drops onto her hand, and shook them off so that they sparkled and flew. "Water." She saw realization dawn in his eyes, and he said something that sounded like "water". "Water," she said again, and nodded encouragingly. "Water," he repeated, more clearly, and both of them smiled. She pointed to herself and said, "Annie." Then, pointing at him, she raised her eyebrows in question. "Ahnaket," he responded. She frowned, puzzled, wondering if he were trying to say her name. He looked at her and said, "Ah-nee," then raised his head a little to look down at himself and said again, "Ahnaket." They looked at each other, and once again they smiled at the dawning of communication between people from alien worlds. She saw that he was young, probably in his twenties, and was amazed again at his competence in the jungle.

When they brought a meal for him, Annie offered to feed him, and the nurse gratefully accepted, looking with fear and distrust at the man in the bed. Annie patiently fed him beef broth, yogurt, and applesauce. She showed him the spoon, the food, and the bowls, saying the words for each slowly and carefully, and each time he tried to repeat them. He asked for water when he wanted some. He seemed to enjoy the flavors of the food, and Annie smacked her lips and asked, "Good?" and he did the same and repeated, "Good". After he had eaten she saw that his eyes were heavy with weariness, and she bent her head and prayed for him, and saw peace in his face as he slipped into sleep. She returned to her own bed tired, and marveling at the blessings of her own life.

The next day she was pronounced well enough to leave the hospital.

"But you must rest only, Miss Robbins. No jungle expeditions, not even any shopping. Not till next week, and then you must come back to the hospital to see the physical therapist before you go anywhere else." Dr Zagad was firm and made her promise. "And you are to come back if you think anything is wrong, if the pain does not diminish. You understand?"

"Yes, Doctor, thank you so much. You have all taken such good care of me." They smiled fondly at her. Her success was their success.

"Annie?" A knock at the door, and a man came in, tall, dark, and handsome, with a voice rich as chocolate as he put out his hand and said, "Tom Williams, Lisha's husband. She sent me to get you. She is running around getting things ready at the house. Oh, and she sent these – she tells me your clothes have bullet holes in them."

She took the bag he gave her into the little bathroom and dressed. The clothes were soft cotton pants, shirt, and flip-flops, easy to put on, and they fit well. Annie marveled again at such friends. The few things she had used at the hospital went into the bag and she was ready.

"Before we go, can we stop by my friend in room 16, please?" she asked, and they went down the hall together. Ahnaket lay staring at the sunlit tree outside his window, but his eyes sparked with recognition again and he said, "Ah-nee" when she entered the room.

"Ahnaket, this is Tom. Tom, this is my friend Ahnaket, who saved our lives in the jungle."

"From what I hear, you saved his when the police were shooting at him," said Tom.

"Oh I don't know about that. Anyway it was pretty silly of me to jump in front of live bullets."

Ahnaket heard the woman speak,
The man answer. He understood
Not the meaning of the speaking, but
That there was meaning if he could learn it.
Had he not learned the woman's words
For the water, the food, the name she was called?
How he would live in this strange world
He knew not. But he was Ahnaket,
A man of the forest people. If he must, he would learn.

Annie tried with gestures to explain that she would be leaving, but that she would return to visit when she was able. She saw that he understood some of what she communicated. She felt that she had a responsibility of trust towards this man who had almost died for her and Katu. She was his only lifeline in an alien world.

Tom drove her to his home in a luxurious Mercedes. The home itself was high on a hill overlooking the city, a mansion of dark brick and white columns, with a sweeping gravel drive out front and a patio and pool out back that took advantage of the views of city and ocean. A buffet lunch had been laid out on the patio, said the uniformed maid, and as they walked through the living room to the open French windows, Annie could hear the sounds of children laughing and splashing in the pool. She stepped outside and caught her breath as she realized the children were Katu and the hunter's baby boy. Lisha came up to them then, laughing and excited. "How do you like my surprise? I told you something came up – it was these two little rascals."

"How – what did you do?" Annie gasped, and at the sound of her voice, Katu swung around and sprang out of the pool, and ran dripping to fling himself at her, laughing and crying, clinging to her as she sat down hard on a nearby chaise.

All through lunch he refused to leave her side, and watched every bite she put in her mouth, as if afraid she were not real and would vanish again. The baby went willingly to anyone who fed him and seemed utterly unperturbed by his strange circumstances.

"So, you wanted to know how we did this? Julak and her sister came with me, and pretended to be the boys' mothers. We went early, before the day shift came on, so the nurses were tired and only too glad to send two rambunctious boys home. Being from the jungle, the women didn't understand anything, and I had to be their interpreter, so it was easy. Well, what do you think?" Lisha beamed with delight.

Annie looked at her friend, remembered how glad she was that she had a friend who knew her way around Bangita, and shook her head. "I probably wouldn't even have thought of it, and if I had I wouldn't have tried it. You never stop amazing me!"

"Yes, Miss Goody Two Shoes, who doesn't believe in a little bribe here and there, you probably wouldn't have thought of it. Well it was a lot of fun, and it still is," she said, smiling fondly at the hunter's baby, who lay sleeping on her lap, his face and hands still sticky with the fruit and bread he had eaten.

"Well," said Tom, rising from the table, "Some of us had better get to work. We can't all chill by the pool all day." He kissed his wife affectionately and said, "I hope I never have to come and bail you out of jail, baby. But you never stop amazing me either."

Part VIII: Restart

He strained to grasp the people's speech.
So many sounds they made! So many
People, so much going and going,
Noise and light even when the
Tree held only darkness in its leaves.
He lay quiet now beneath their hands when they
Touched his wounds, brought
Food and water. The woman Ah-nee worked
Magic with the people; she came, and
She spoke much with them, and also with him,
And they saw him now
Without hatred. He sat upright.
No longer was he restrained as before,
For they saw that he no longer struggled to flee.
She brought sometimes a woman,
Sometimes a man. They spoke together in their
Strange tongue. One day they brought to him
The boy, his son, who came to him and touched him,
Touched him with his baby hands,
And petted his face with his baby fingers,
And laughed with great joy to see him. His eyes
Overflowed, and he felt the water on his cheeks
That unmanned him. He saw
That the faces of Ah-nee and her friends were wet also,
And that it mattered not at all.

It seemed to him then, that this
Was a woman for him, and a

Mother for his child, and that
For this purpose she had come.
The slaying of the cat proved only
That he was worthy of her, a protector
For her and the children in her care.
He thought much on this, watched her
When she came, saw the
Tenderness with which she spoke to him.
She was scarred, yes, and that strange pale color;
Still, she was a woman, and had a woman's
Appeal, beneath the strange garments. He
Settled in his mind to take her for his woman
After the custom of his people
When healing came; then
Return with her to the place
Of the forest people.

The healing came slowly, strength returned
Slowly. They made him stand, practice
Walking, gave him the tools for eating so that
He might feed himself. There was a cold, white cave
With a small waterfall to make oneself clean.
The water was warm and pleasant. One could also
Purge one's body and clean everything with water.
The noise of it startled. It pleased the people
That he should use their white cave,
So he did so. They gave him soft skins for a loincloth.
He wrapped himself with the skins from the bed
Against the cold of the place they were in,
Cold such as he had never known in the jungle.

He was a man, a strong man. He would learn
The ways of these people, as he knew the ways
Of his jungle world.

"Lisha, my brother is in Bangita City," Annie said. She was holding a letter in her hands, and the expression on her face was of stunned disbelief.

"What? What are you saying?" Lisha came and stood beside her, peering over her shoulder to decipher the doctor's scrawl on the page.

Trying to pull the lost threads of her life together, Annie had had no difficulty convincing Lisha to help her track down any of her belongings that might still be in BC. They had gone to the embassy to arrange for a new passport. Mr. Grant's aide, who remembered Annie well, told them that Ben was away at college, and that his parents were unavailable. More than that, she said, she was unable to say for security reasons. She hoped they would understand.

They had gone to the bank, where Annie explained that she had lost all her bank cards and her passport, and Lisha had sworn that she was who said she was, and she had been able to withdraw some money to buy some clothes and other necessities while they prepared another debit card for her.

At the Palmers' former home, the homeowner rather grumpily hauled a box out of the garage, into which he had thrown anything he had found lying about the house when he moved in. Far as he knew it was just junk, he said, but they were welcome to it. He was just happy to be rid of it, though he also seemed happy enough to take the dollar bills Lisha offered him for his trouble.

At the former mission office, the new tenants cheerfully pulled out a bundle of mail tied up in string, which, they said, they hadn't wanted to throw away in case someone ever came to collect it, and see, they had been right all the time! And, oh yes, someone had found a laptop computer in one of the back rooms, that was no use to them because it was password protected, and they weren't good hackers. It had the initials AR written on it somewhere. Was it theirs?

And now Annie sat reading letters, sorted into date order by their post office stamps, sent to her by Aunt Ginny, by Charlie, and by Ben. When she saw them she was shaken by such powerful emotion that she wasn't sure if she would actually be able to read them. She had taken a walk around the patio, breathing deeply, before she felt able to sit in a quiet place and read.

Aunt Ginny had sent her loving greetings and a Christmas card. The old lady's handwriting was so shaky that it was barely legible, and

Annie was troubled, feeling she would very likely never see her again. And in fact one of Charlie's letters, written in January, confirmed that their aunt had passed away peacefully in her sleep one night soon after Christmas. Annie's heart ached and she wept for her loss.

Charlie's monthly letters, chatty at first, showed growing concern for her as the months went by with no response from Bangita. He had completed the last of his internship requirements, written his last paper, taken his final comprehensive examination, and was now a medical doctor. And, said his last letter, written in May, he would be coming out to Bangita after the lease on his apartment expired. His relationship with Ashley hadn't worked out, he had sold his car and a few possessions, and with the rest he would be moving to Bangita City, where he would be able to practice medicine and keep an eye on his little sister at the same time. He expected to arrive in the first week of June.

"He must have been here for weeks already – it's the end of June! How can I find him? Where could he be?"

"Girl, you panic way too much. Just think it through! First of all, we could just call all the hospitals and medical practices in town to see where he is working, but that'll take some time. So, is there any place you wrote him about that we haven't been yet?"

"Well, I wrote about church, the Palmers, the mission office... I wrote about Mama Deem's. Perhaps he went there? But he wouldn't stay there – he must be living in town somewhere."

"Okay, but let's try this Mama Deem's and see if they've seen him. Where is this and how come we haven't been there yet?"

"Oh, it's in Falaga, we couldn't go there, not by ourselves. I think I might even get lost, though I went there with Ben a lot."

"Don't be telling me where we can and can't go, girl. You should know me by now. Come on, there's no time like the present." And she got up off the sofa and began to put on her shoes.

"But we can't take your car, Lisha! Your Mercedes! You don't know this place! It's awful!"

Lisha gave her that look only she could give. "Okay, then, I'll ask Julak if I can borrow her car. She can take mine to the store. She'll like that. She has a Volkswagen – is that suitable for Falaga?"

Annie was still experiencing near panic, but managed to nod. She went to collect her purse and her shoes. They arranged the car swap with Julak and she promised to watch the boys, and they were on their way to Mama Deem's.

Annie was able to remember the way with only one minor detour. They arrived at the familiar building and honked, as Ben always did, and Marteya's face appeared at the window. Then Marteya herself stepped through the little door in the wall. Annie stumbled awkwardly out of the car and they hugged and cried for joy at seeing one another again.

"We have waited and waited for you, Annie, and now at last you are here. Come in! Come in!"

They opened the door so that Lisha could drive Julak's grey Volkswagen into the familiar courtyard. Annie felt that she had come home.

Lisha had become unusually quiet as they drove through Falaga and she still seemed subdued as she looked about her. The women preparing the evening meal called out cheerful greetings. The children played and shouted happily on the floor. Mama Deem's chair was empty.

"Mama is not so well," Marteya told them. "We wanted to take her to the hospice, where she could receive better care, but she says, why would she want to be anywhere else but here? I will see if she feels strong enough for visitors."

"Marteya, has my brother been here?"

Without replying Marteya led the way down the hallway towards the bedroom area and into a small, sparsely furnished room. Mama Deem lay on a bed in the corner, her frail body making a tiny mound under the bedclothes, and Charlie rose from a chair by her bedside.

There was so much to be said that at first they said nothing, only held each other and cried and laughed together. Then Charlie stepped back, his hands on Annie's shoulders, and she saw the doctor and the older brother examine her with growing concern.

"Annie, what has happened to you?" His fingers brushed back her hair and gently probed the scars and puckered skin of her face.

She told him the story as they talked and ate together, sharing the children's meal in the main dining area. Charlie lifted Mama's frail body in his arms and carried her like a baby to her chair. Propped and padded with pillows and blankets, she was able to enjoy their family time as Marteya helped her eat. Lisha, still remarkably quiet, barely ate as she fussed over the little ones, feeding them, wiping little faces and hands, and helping to clean up a spill on the floor. At nap time she disappeared with the other women to change diapers and put the little ones in bed. In a while they heard someone singing a sweet gentle lullaby.

"That's so lovely," said Annie. "Do you sing to the children every day?"

"Oh no," said Marteya, "none of us can sing like that - it must be your friend Lisha. What a lovely voice!"

"I didn't know she could sing so beautifully. I guess there's a lot I don't know about her," Annie said. She turned to Charlie and told him how Lisha had claimed the boys from the hospital.

"I've been thinking so much about Takatu and the Kinta people. They must have given us up for dead a long time ago. Can you think of any way we can get hold of a four-wheel-drive and get Katu back to his parents?"

"Actually I have exactly the thing you need. I bought an old Land Rover and it's in the shop for a brake job. I think it really needs to take a trip into the jungle to make sure everything's working right. What do you say, Marteya, do you want to come?" Annie looked from Charlie to Marteya and back again and saw the spark of affection in both of their faces. *Oh, that's interesting*, she thought. She felt a little flush of pleasure at the thought of her brother and her friend together.

"That sounds great – when can we go?" Marteya's eyes sparkled with pleasure. She was seldom able to leave home; her physical and financial handicaps constrained her world.

They both looked at Annie with raised eyebrows. "The sooner, the better – how about tomorrow?" suggested Annie eagerly. "What do we need to do to make it happen?" They began eagerly to plan their trip.

When Lisha returned with the other women they embarrassed her by admiring her singing.

"Man, I didn't know you could hear me! Those kids are too much – I just want to take them all home with me."

"Lisha, Charlie can take us to Kinta tomorrow, so we can take Katu back to his mom," said Annie excitedly. "I don't think I'm ready to stay there yet, though we should probably plan on staying overnight. At least they will know that we're alive and he can be with his family again. You want to come too, don't you?"

"Try to stop me! What a trip! I've never been into the jungle at all – at least not the kind of place you're talking about." A little sadness crept over her features. "I'm gonna miss that little rascal, that's for sure, but he needs to be with his mama. I can't even imagine what she must be going through."

Later that evening, in the guest room at Lisha and Tom's home, Annie saw the letters she had left on the table when they had hurried off to Falaga. There were two letters from Ben. She held them in her hands for a long time, afraid to open them for what she might read. Afraid of how she might respond. She saw that one of them had been mailed in Bangita City in December. The second one was mailed in June from an address in the US. She breathed a prayer as she opened the earlier one first.

Bangita City, December

Dear Annie,

I heard that you went home to the US with the Palmers – I was sorry not to have been able to see you and apologize in person. I wanted to ask you to forgive me for being angry and raging at God.

I also want to say that I meant what I said: I love you and would consider it a great honor to spend the rest of my life with you. If you should ever feel the same way, and decide that a relationship with me is a God-thing, please let me know in some way. I will be praying for you and also for humility to accept whatever He decides. In the meantime, I hope that we can at least be friends when you return from the States.

Your friend in love,
Ben

Annie sat for a long time with the little letter in her hand, wondering at the ways that people miss each other in their efforts to communicate. She got up and rummaged through the box of "junk" from the Palmers' house. In a bag of papers, bills, and flyers, months out of date, she found the card she had written and left for Ben with such mixed emotions. It was unopened. She turned to the second letter.

My dearest Annie,

Nothing that has happened, no one I have met, has made me change my mind about what I wrote to you in December, except finding out a few days ago that in fact you had not gone back to the US but went back to Kinta village. Then I regretted writing at all, and not coming out to see you many times in the months since then. Especially when I heard about Mr. Palmer's death and realized what that has meant for you. You must wonder how I could have remained so ignorant, but I admit I have avoided the church and have taken assignments away from the city as much as possible for the past six months.

In the meantime I made plans to return to my father's alma mater to do post-grad work in nature conservation. My father's parents are retiring and coming to live with us in Bangita when I have finished my studies. I will be spending the summer with them, helping them as they sell their hardware store and pack for the move.

I came to Kinta to say goodbye when I found out you were there, but when I arrived you had been lost in the jungle for two days. We have searched for you and I am afraid for your safety, but I can't see how God would allow you to die in the jungle. Perhaps I am in denial. Still, I am hoping and believing that somehow, one day, you will get this letter and will perhaps write to me. You will always be a flame in the darkness for me, and I remain

Your friend in love
Ben

The boy saw the unfamiliar change slowly to familiar, as the city's confusing conglomerate of buildings, roads, people, and vehicles fell behind them. Small tracts of greenery gave way to the jungle. The vast green was alive in his mind with every shade and nuance of leaf and twig, creeping and breathing and edible and dangerous, readable to him as a city child's comic book. He began to breathe deeper and gradually his excitement mounted until he was rattling off information to his back-seat companions in bewildering rapid-fire like an over-caffeinated tour guide.

Only when they turned off the paved highway onto the rutted mud roads that led to his home did the boy finally grow quiet, as he felt a tide of emotion swell till it threatened to burst his carefully constructed defenses. A real man could not weep at the sight of his home and his people, surely, yet why should he feel this pain in his throat? They took turn after turn, Ah-nee remembering and showing her brother the ways to go. The roads grew ever smaller till at the last they were pushing between tall clumps of grass and overhanging branches that screeched down the sides of the jeep and finally they were there. They were out of the thick green walls and there was Kinta. There were his people, standing frozen in place and waiting for what they would see when the noise they had heard from far away finally arrived.

Then he was out of the vehicle, scrambling and clambering over Lisha's lap to fling himself at his mother and little sister. As she saw him his mother's face grew suddenly pale and her eyes rolled in some strange way and her legs folded beneath her and she fell, though the arms of those around her caught and held her and lowered her gently to the ground. *Mama,* he cried, and tried to lift her in his arms, and her eyes fluttered open and he saw such a smile on her face as he had never seen before. It mattered not that the tears flowed from his eyes because as he looked around him he saw that the face of every man, woman, and child was wet also.

The other travelers climbed out of the vehicle and suddenly there was a storm of wild ululation as the people of Kinta engulfed Katu and Annie in a sea of loving embraces. The men's faces were split in the widest grins ever seen and they greeted Charlie as a long lost brother – the man who had returned their lost people to them.

For a few minutes of chaos Lisha and Marteya were left standing observing and then Aheyla, the headman's wife, remembered her manners and turned to greet them in Bangese. Annie realized what was happening and turned to help.

"My friends," she addressed the Kinta people in Bangese, "This is my family – my brother Charlie and my sisters Lisha and Marteya." Then in English, "Guys, this is my Kinta village family," and she began to name them, one by one, and to cry and laugh together with them at the joy of knowing such love and community.

Suddenly people were scurrying in all directions to prepare food for a party that would certainly last all night. The men swept Charlie and Katu up in their midst and soon the frantic bleating of goats announced the selection of the main course. Women could be seen gathering baskets of vegetables from their gardens and setting cooking pots over their fires. Young boys busily swept the gathering place and carried in armloads of firewood. Soon the air was redolent with scented wood smoke and enticing smells of cooking food.

Little girls appeared with bunches of wildflowers and sweet-scented herbs in their hands, and a group of the leading women escorted Annie and her friends to her hut, where they removed dried remnants of vines and creepers that hung over the doorway. Aheyla explained to them that they had hung the trailing plants as a symbol of mourning and that they would now hang flowers as a symbol of birth. They began to decorate the little hut with sprigs of fresh greenery, woven carefully into the thatch, and carried out Annie's possessions to brush and clean them and shake the dust from her blankets and mats. Aheyla directed operations and insisted that Annie and her sisters not do anything but allow themselves to be hung about with flowers and garlands of herbs. The hut took on a festive air. The women began to nudge and whisper to one another and one of them went inside and brought out Annie's guitar. They asked her to play for them. As she tuned the instrument she felt the tears spring to her eyes and they sang together the little songs she had taught them, most imperfectly through their tears and laughter. Around the village, people stopped to listen; then they smiled and hummed along with the familiar tunes.

It was a party to end all parties. Katu told his friends the story of their adventures over and over many times and each time the jungle was hotter and more dangerous, their way longer and more torturous, and his part more heroic than the time before. The cat grew into a monstrous creature and the hunter was a fearsome giant with a spear as tall as a tree. Batah and the other boys listened with wide eyes, all the while pretending not to believe a word. Marteya and Annie translated for Lisha and Charlie, as everyone tried to find out about the world where Annie's odd family came from, where sisters looked nothing at all alike. They ate and drank and danced and sang and talked until they were overcome with sleep. They trailed off to bed as the birds began to call the rising sun, the men to the men's hut, Lisha and Marteya with Annie to hers, sweetly scented with flower garlands in the predawn.

"No wonder you loved it here, Annie," said Marteya softly as they lay on the sleeping mats. "They are your family."

Journal Entry: Bangita City

It's so good to have my journal again; though my head and my heart are both so full I'm not sure where to begin. Going back to Kinta was surreal, especially because Charlie and Lisha and Marteya were with me. It was also wonderful, because the Kinta people made me feel so welcome. They even seemed disappointed when I left with the others, which is just so confusing after the way they didn't want me before. People are strange - but I can't help loving them anyway.

Charlie and I have been talking about the future. All our former ties seem to have been cut. We have only each other for family and nothing to go back to the States for. It seems highly likely that he will have every reason to stay, if his relationship with Marteya continues to grow. Mama Deem is so ill that Mama Besh is running Shamah-Abeh. Lisha is there every day. I don't know the story about why she has no kids of her own, but mothering all these lost little ones is bringing her so much happiness. She is such a blessing to Mama Besh and the other ladies, to say nothing of the children!

We all want to stay connected to Kinta and Charlie is looking at the possibility of starting a clinic up there. There are a lot of hoops to jump through to get him certified to practice medicine here. I took him to see Dr. Zagad, who was very pleased to find out that I'm not a complete orphan and even more pleased when Charlie said he was available to help at the hospital. They seem to be working out some sort of internship deal for him that will help with getting his medical status sorted out. I didn't know this before, but Charlie took some classes in tropical medicine when he knew I was coming out to Bangita. It's so amazing how God works things out.

Tomorrow Ahnaket can leave the hospital. None of us is quite sure what we should do about him. We don't feel like we can just drive up to the jungle and drop him off and say, Bye, have a nice life! He still needs some recovery time and of course there's his little boy, who doesn't seem to have a name. Tom started calling him "Mowgli" after Kipling's character and that's stuck for now, but presumably he has another name that we just haven't heard yet? For now, Tom and Lisha say they can stay here with them. They are the most hospitable people I've ever met.

As I look back at my earlier entries in this book, I see how much has happened and how much I have changed, all the people I've met that have become part of my life, and the way Bangita is home to me in *so many ways. I have no idea what I will be doing in the next couple of years, but I can't imagine what I would do if I went back to the States now either. Problem is, if I don't get things sorted out soon, my visa will expire and then I will have to leave. God, what do you want me to do? Was all of this really your will for me? Even bizarre things like getting shot? If I am not a missionary to Kinta, who am I? That's how I saw myself for so long, yet I never really was that. We get so stuck on having a label that describes what we do; then we say that's who we are, but really we are so much more than that. Mama Deem never really DID anything except love babies, but she is definitely someone. What's going on inside of me is who I really am. It's my soul that matters, more than the outward stuff, and who I am towards God. That hasn't changed, except maybe to go deeper. Even though some of my ideas about God have changed, He is more real to me than ever before.*

Mama Deem's frail body weighed very little; the heaviness of the coffin had much to do with the weight of sorrow and love and gratitude the people carried in their hearts as they bore her on foot over the rutted roads of Falaga to the burial place of the poor. Her children, the grown men and women who lived only because she had loved another tiny baby into adulthood, keened and wept freely as they took turns to carry a casket so loaded with flowers, pictures, and mementoes that it could barely be seen. There were people of every color and size and social standing in her train, but even the youngest and the poorest held their heads high with that confidence that comes of having been loved by the ones who raised you.

At the graveside a hot wind teased the red earth into stinging dust devils. The people stood with sweat trickling down their temples and the hollows of their spines, but still each one had a tribute, a song, or a poem to be read. None felt ready to leave that red hillside where nothing grew but worn, lopsided wooden crosses and ragged, poorly carved headstones.

At last the singing died away. One of the preachers raised his arms and offered a final prayer of benediction and gratitude and as the sighed amen swept the crowd, the casket was lowered into the waiting earth and the first clods of dirt thumped onto its lid. Loving hands gently tossed the sun-warmed granules until the red-earth blanket was piled high and then loaded with the flowers and love-notes. Still the people stood uncertainly by, while the sun sank lower and the wind went to rest. Finally the tremulous query of a hungry child somewhere in the crowd drew them back and they began to drift silently away, each one holding their memories as treasure in their hearts. For what can we know of another's soul?

Part IX: Destinations

They came one day, Ah-nee and her friends,
And brought with them some garments such as they wore.
With gestures and more words they showed him
That he, Ahnaket, should put on the garments.
The man showed him how to arrange the loincloth,
And a soft garment for his upper body
It seemed strange to him to be covered,
To feel the soft rub of the skins on his skin.
From which animals they had taken the skins
He could not imagine.
There were garments for his feet also.
Though he had never worn such things before,
It seemed better than the cold smooth
Stone where they walked.
They led him away down long tunnels,
Smooth cool caves filled with light
And people walking, talking. There were
Voices in the walls of the cave. There were
Sleeping mats with legs and round feet
That moved when pushed, carrying
More people, wounded and sick people.
There were many, many people.
They entered a small cave and stood together;
Lights blinked in the walls of the cave;
Music and voices came and went.
The cave moved beneath their feet; the walls
Opened and closed and people
Came in and went out. Still

Ah-nee and her friends stood calmly,
Talking their strange talk, unperturbed.
So he stood quiet, trusting them,
Till they too, went out; he
Followed. They talked with
More people, who worked with things
That hummed and clicked and made
Great white leaves, which the man
Tahm took and folded into his garments.
They went towards a place where he could see
Bright sunlight and trees; large shining beasts with
Round feet carried more people.
Ah-nee and Tahm and Tahm's woman Lee-shah
Walked to one of the shining beasts.
They opened it. They got inside of it and sat.
They beckoned to him to follow, so he crept
Inside the beast. It had a strange smell,
A smell akin to that of the Tree-Eaters.
The smell made a hard knot in his belly.
Inside the beast was both soft and hard.
He crouched inside. Tahm
Made the beast roar and move
And carry them a great distance, at a speed far greater
Than the fastest hunter could run.

They passed many houses, that
Shone in the bright sun, and more people
Than he had imagined existed.
Many of the houses had designs
Or pictures painted on them. The people went
In and out, in and out, carrying things that made no sense.
The people were of every shade and hue of brown
Or the pale color of Ah-nee.
There were trees, but none of the great ones of the forest.
Few animals he saw, small and of no good
Eating. On what did these many people
Feast? Could there be enough animals in all the forest
To make just one meal for so many?

He rode in the beast and stared
Until his eyes hurt with staring.

He squatted there in the belly of the beast
And laid his head on his knees. He
Wrapped his arms about his head and
Covered his eyes and his ears and dreamed
Of forests and running water and the sounds
Of monkey, bird, and insect.

Journal Entry: Ahnaket

I'm writing to try to help me sort out my thoughts and feelings. We brought Ahnaket back to Tom and Lisha's from the hospital a few days ago and he has really struggled to fit in to this way of life. Things like sitting on chairs, going into bedrooms to sleep, cooking food in a modern kitchen with cabinets and a stove and dishwasher, and wearing clothes, are unthinkable to him. Then there's the food itself, let alone the dishes we use.

Then there was last night. He came into my room after we had all gone to bed. Thankfully I was reading so my light was still on. He started trying to speak to me about something, saying, "Come!" so I got up, and he grabbed my arm and said something about Annie and Ahnaket, and gesturing from himself to me, and started pulling me towards the door. I didn't know what he was trying to say (so naive!), so I went with him into the hallway and then he wanted me to go into his room with him, but I pulled away, so he grabbed me and pulled me into his room and started trying to pull off his clothes with one hand and pushing me towards the bed. I tried to go but he is so strong! But I got away and ran into my room and locked the door. And cried of course. I was so scared.

This morning no one knew where he was. They all knew there was something wrong with me too, but I just couldn't tell them. Eventually the gardener came in and said that the jungle man was sitting up in a tree. It was such a mess. Tom figured out what was going on when he saw my face and he laughed and said, Oh he's sulking because Annie doesn't want him! Lisha saw that I was upset and she was mad at Ahnaket, but kind of amused too I think.

Anyway they're realizing he won't be able to stay here forever and we will have to figure out how to get him back to the jungle or SOMETHING.

From the height of the tree,
In wounded pride and confusion of soul,
He gazed with longing
At distant mountains, softly furred in green.
He must leave this alien world,
Where things were not as they seemed.
But what of his child?
A baby needed women.
He, Ahnaket, needed no woman.

That evening the doe-eyed daughter of Julak coaxed him from the tree and sat with him on the grass while he ate the dinner she had brought him. With her shy smile and sidelong glances she made him feel that perhaps a woman was a pleasant companion after all. And a woman who would bring a man such food? He laughed at the thought of all he was learning.

Letter: October

Dear Ben,

I finally got your letter just a few weeks ago. I wanted to write before but wasn't really sure what to say. So much has happened, but I wanted you know that I am well. I will be going back to Kinta and starting the school at last. My visa has been renewed at the request of the Kinta people. We will also be starting a clinic in Kinta.

You may have heard that Mama Deem died last month. Hers was the most amazing funeral I have ever been to. It was an honor to know her - thank you for taking me to meet her.

Thank you for being a wonderful friend. If you are ever near Kinta again, it would be good to see you.

Always your friend,
Annie

He left the Jeep in a tiny clearing about a mile from the main village and walked the rest of the way, remembering with shame his mad entrance the last time he was here; so he came to the village clearing unnoticed and stood for a few minutes watching the scenes of activity before him. He saw that the women were tending their gardens on the other side of the clearing. Even from a distance he could hear their calls and laughter faintly on the little breeze that cooled his skin. He noticed a large hut near the meeting place that hadn't been there before. There seemed to be a lot of people standing around nearby.

Then one of the bending women stood up and drew her headscarf from her hair. There was no mistaking the flash of that golden hair or the ripple of laughter that reached across the distance and made his spine tingle. He stepped forward, about to go to her, when a voice called out, *It is Ben!*

Smiling men and children surrounded him, greeting him with laughter and joy in their eyes, saying, *She is here, she is here, come and see!* So many other things were being told him at once that he could not understand any of it, but Katu was running across the clearing, children streaming in his wake, calling to Annie, *Come, come at once, come and see!*

The men drew him towards the meeting place and he began to understand that they were telling him they had a clinic now. He saw a tall man with sandy blond hair step out of the big hut and look around, puzzled at the commotion. He had on a white coat and a stethoscope was draped around his neck – the new doctor, apparently. The doctor beckoned to the next person waiting for him and they went back inside.

And here was Annie, escorted by a horde of excited children all babbling at once. She was blushing and clearly embarrassed by the fuss, but she looked up at him steadily as she drew near.

"Hey Ben," she said in her lovely voice.

He saw the reserve in her eyes and he realized why it was there, as she lifted her hand and drew her hair behind her ear. He saw the scars and his heart turned over as he realized how close they had come to losing her. She saw the shock in his face and dropped her eyes, hurt and disappointed. He stepped forward and took her reluctant hand in his own; he lifted it to his lips and kissed it gently and held it in both of his. She remembered the first time they had met and lifted her eyes to his, expecting rejection and repugnance. She found joy and love and tenderness.

"Annie, we almost lost you!" his voice was whisper soft and barely audible amid the chorus of giggling and throat-clearing that erupted around them. Startled, she pulled her hand from his. They laughed, embarrassed, and stepped back from the cultural faux pas.

The crowd parted as the blond-haired doctor came up to Annie and put his hand on her shoulder. Ben's heart dropped as he thought of who this man might be to her. Annie looked from one to the other and said, "Charlie, this is Ben – I told you about him."

Charlie reached out a large hand and shook Ben's.

"Pleased to meet you, Ben," Charlie said. He stood with his head on one side, considering Ben's conflicted face. "You needn't look so miserable. I'm her brother."

The relief they saw on Ben's face was so palpable that everyone laughed. Ben saw Annie's eyes brighten. She saw his eyebrows lift and the unspoken question that hung in his anxious eyes. A happy smile grew across her face.

"Yes, Ben," she said. "Yes."

ABOUT THE AUTHOR

Mary Paynter grew up in South Africa and has lived in Georgia, Iowa, Florida, South Carolina and Kansas. Someone who knows how different those places can be from one another will understand why she has observed and experienced many cross-cultural mishaps. They can be painful. Most are just plain funny.

Made in the USA
Charleston, SC
25 August 2015